A Year in Ink

VOLUME 5

A Year in Ink

San Diego Writers, Ink
ANTHOLOGY
VOLUME 5

Edited by Brandon Cesmat and T. Greenwood

THE
INK SPOT
PRESS
San Diego, California

A Year in Ink is a publication of
Ink Spot Press
San Diego Writers, Ink
PO Box 34374
San Diego, CA 92163

First Readers: Daniel Amato, Scott Barbour, Judith Barkley, Osanna
Bennett, Marivi Soliven Blanco, Jackie Bouchard, Kaitlin Brooks,
Michelle Campbell, Tina Coffey, Janice Coy, Sumilu Cue, Stephanie
Doyle, Melody Fleetwood, Shary Folkman, Michele Galper, Shonna
Gillis, Hilary Grimes, Serenity Harding, Randy Herman, Leslie
Hodge, Kathie Hoxsie, Rebecca Johnson, Kirsten Kessler, Anita
Knowles, Randall Lahrman, Sylvia Levinson, John MacDonald,
Stacy Magic, Barbara McMikle, Rachel Moore, Roselyn O'Connell,
Megan Pappas, Sabrina Pettis, Brendan Praniewicz, Khojesta
Price, Deborah Ramos, Ely Rareshide, Judy Reeves, Maggi Roark,
Deborah Serra, Marg Wafer and Matthew Williams

Editorial Committee: John MacDonald with Dipthi Battipadi, Puja
Bhanot, Megan Elliot, Rachel Moore and Margaret Wafer

Cover art: Sparklers, ©2007 T. Greenwood

Design and typography: Armadillo Creative

ISBN 978-0-9799204-5-5

Printed in the United States of America
Printed by Lightning Source Inc.

Contents

Introduction by Brandon Cesmat

If titles count, *A Year in Ink* is about what the writers who tumbled into the extreme southwest corner of the U.S. decided to submit halfway through 2011. No more, no less. And that's enough.

It's not easy writing in San Diego. I don't want to name names, but we are the town that proved "New York, New York" wrong: just because you can fake it there doesn't mean you can fake it anywhere. As poet John Peterson noted, you can tell San Diego isn't really a part of the rest of the U.S. because of the extra set of immigration check points at the county line on I-5, I-15 & I-8; it gives the impression no one wants to hear what we have to say. A calendar of "Southern California Poetry" managed to name 48 poets without one San Diegueño among them. A careful reading of certain "California" poetry anthologies shows that one of the best career moves a San Diego poet could make would be to relocate to San Francisco and die.

So what's a San Diegueño writer to do? Write and publish. In a previous edition of *A Year in Ink*, former *Union Tribune* books editor Arthur Salm wrote, "I confess to being a contrarian [when] it comes to the literal idea of writers as a literal, physical community... But a figurative, literary community? Oh, yes, indeed." One good confession deserves another: any community that doesn't manifest some point-at-able aesthetics is not a community, but a multitude waiting for a miracle. It's not just the bound pages, but what's on them that matters. Oh me of little faith.

So what are the significant poetics of San Diego? In these pages, can a regional accent be heard? Do the form and content of these poems resonate with this time and place? Most of these poems have right margins like the coastline if you're facing Tijuana. Sorry, neo-formalists. These lines break where image or music need to; it's a border thing. It's a form manifest. And it's neo every day.

Reading submissions, I did discover a consistent characteristic: most have nothing to do with San Diego during or around 2011. Yet

1

2011 was an astonishing year in this old city. The ocean that largely defines it changed. A cold current came ashore farther north than it had in the past, bringing with it black jellyfish that drove swimmers from the water. A photograph of a large fin among surfers in Cardiff went viral and raised discussions about sharks frequenting our coast. A band of Kumeyaay Indians put the name of their casino on the old Sports Arena, just off the historic Kumeyaay Trail to Playas (now called "Rosecrans Street"). The Pala Band of Indians continued their battle to purchase back their ancestral homelands in Warner Springs, a volta in the poem of history.

Poetry, however, favors an intimate persona over a public one. The whispering of subtext can't always be heard in the public voice of "we."

In poetry, saying something while making it sound interesting is risky business. In a poem like "jazz is e.e. cummings," if the poet can run a line of euphonic imagery in one direction, pivot without losing flow and avoid running in the ruts of the literal, it will be fine. We like our music imbued with more than sound. Poems like "Silent Movie," "What the World Sounds" and "Why I Married Him" all have that music and luminous imagery that draws me.

In a sense, "Why I Married Him" is a solid representative of San Diego poems: first, it has nothing to do with San Diego; second, it's about leaving someplace (in this case, Milwaukee); and third, the poem ended up here. Most importantly for me it eschews the obvious and finds awe:

> I lived without music then, cut off
> from the Rain Prelude and nocturnes
> of fog, but the bridge! It buzzed –
> no, not like a giant bumblebee,
> but only as a metal bridge can sing,
> from the maws of Bethlehem Steel.

"Familia Anclada" (anchor family) is another poem about leaving or at least needing to leave. It's a poem that doesn't offer an answer but raises the right questions.

> She cannot cross the desert
> with her babies,
> The able kids are throwing gang signs
> in the alleys littered in crime scenes

In "What I Know," Red-necked Phalaropes stop over at Mono Lake on their way here. The birders walk in "single file" on the path through the rare environment: "each soft step/we take in this tender landscape/says we wish to be nowhere else."

So does each poem in this anthology. At least for 2011.

This anthology represents a community, a point of culmination from many directions. One morning in The Ink Spot, Kelli Wescott, T. Greenwood and I sat around that big table upstairs while the fierce sun lit the poems and prose. Kelli kept track as Tammy and I introduced pieces to each other, like planning a dinner party: "Seat this chapter beside this poem because they have a lot in common to converse about."

So cook last year and cancel the calendar. This place of pages is rocking, and it looks as if we're going to party for the rest of the night.

— Brandon Cesmat, Poetry Editor 2011

Introduction by
T. Greenwood

This is why I love leading adult writing workshops.

This, *here*, this collection of beautiful, aching, heart-breaking, funny, and wise stories. These characters' lives made vivid on the page in lyrical or deliciously economical prose. These glorious explorations and illustrations of lust and loneliness, fear and frustration. These ruminations on the complexity of our lives, or the simple lovely rendering of a midnight conversation.

I love teaching adult writers because adult writers have known love (really, really known love) and the loss of it. They have hurt and ached and longed. They have married and divorced; they have had children and lost parents. They have worked as labor organizers and lawyers, nurses and neurologists, stunt women and animal trainers. They are musicians and artists and architects. They are mothers and fathers. In short, they have lived fascinating lives, and have decided, for whatever reason, to channel all of that human yearning and experience into poetry or prose.

My favorite writing prompt is "I write because..." This exercise forces authors to articulate the driving force behind their writing. It makes them think about this choice, this brave decision to etch their lives on the page. *I write because I love words. I write for attention. For posterity. For revenge. I write because I am afraid to speak. I write to make people laugh, to make myself laugh so that I will not cry. I write for my children. I write to survive.* Whatever the reason, my adult students and colleagues at SDWI, while as diverse in background and education and culture as any I have ever seen, all share this passion and compulsion for writing.

The anonymous selection process for this anthology was nerve wracking, because with each story, I imagined the joy or sorrow my decision would cause for these authors. I also thought about the lives behind the stories, how the slivers of truth that acted as each story's spark revealed the greater truths of each author's life. I was admittedly relieved, and thrilled, to find that my selections included several of the authors who have sat with me at my workshop table.

I was also excited that there were so many voices I didn't know yet that spoke to me in such resounding voices.

There were many, many beautiful stories that I had to let go in favor of others. The editorial process is an agonizing one—as anyone who writes knows—and there were many, many darlings killed in my selection process. But I also believe that I have chosen the best of the best, representing and honoring that eclectic, wonderful diversity found on any given Saturday (or Monday or Wednesday or Sunday) inside the walls of The Ink Spot. And I only hope that I have done justice to these myriad stories and their authors' shared passion for prose.

— T. Greenwood, Prose Editor 2011

The Ward

Eber Lambert

*T*he old man lying in the next bed talked in his sleep, telling stories of anxious villains and fallen heroes from fallen wars. His voice would vary: sometimes that of a pompous Ivy League historian, or with a glib drawl of a southern preacher, and other times that of a nasal monotone radio sportscaster, as if calling a scoreless mid-July Mets game. Sometimes his stories were delivered in third person narration—he the dutiful reporter of fact and occasional expository sidebar. Other times they were crafted as levelheaded memoir in full character with emotional extremes consistently kept in line. He would drift into mumbles every so often but return reinvigorated within minutes with an inspired stream rife with detail and flowery prose. He never fell silent for more than five or ten minutes, and as far as I could glean from the occasional comments by the nurses, he was never awake. Meanwhile I—though thoroughly captivated by his storytelling—had just the opposite problem: I had not slept since being transferred in here from the ER three days before.

There were about twenty of us crammed in the supposedly sterile level-four isolation of the Highly Infectious Disease Ward, arranged in two long rows of narrow, stainless-steel-framed beds like cadavers in an anatomy lab. I never actually saw the storytelling old man, only his bare, bony feet. A splatter-stained vinyl curtain was partially drawn between us, butting up against a shared rack of diagnostic monitors blipping and humming away, reporting heart rate, respiratory stats, and our basic will-to-live quotients.

After two days of listening to his continuous series of adventures spanning the major frontiers, prohibition era crime stories, and seemingly every armed conflict of western culture for the past 1200 years, he finally slurred and stuttered his way into almost an hour of extended silence. I assumed he had paused to refill his hundred-gallon syllable tank but also feared he might rewind to the beginning. At first, I welcomed the break. It allowed me to stop listening and catch up on my clock and ceiling staring. But soon I realized that his stories were keeping my frenetic mind in check, and in their absence I became agitated, knotted tightly around my relentless insomnia.

At exactly midnight, the old man resumed. His voice was noticeably different than any he had employed previously. Though loud enough to hear, it was gentle, soft-spoken. It took a minute or so before he revealed that he was speaking in the voice of a woman name Aysa. Her English was broken: her vocabulary very simple, in a thick accent unfamiliar and oddly primitive. She spent several minutes on her genealogy, listing ancient sounding names I had never heard of. She finally announced that she lived 11,000 years ago and claimed to be the common ancestor of nearly one-fourth of today's population. Her people were the descendants of the Sun God Utu, living in the village of Vadu in ancient Sumer along the southern Tigris River. She described the grass and mud hut she shared with three younger women and their small children, and that she had spent most of her life carrying water from the river, tending the fire and grinding wild rice on a sacred stone. She bore six children of her own, all now grown, from three different fathers, all now dead, her oldest child fathered by her own father. The previous night, she said, marked the 500th full moon of her life, which meant that she was required to leave the village, travel for eight days into the mountains of the sunset in search of a place to die.

Coming to a waterfall, she chanted as the sunlight refracted into multiple concentric rainbows in the mist. As the evening arrived, she gathered up a couple dozen stones and tied them into her tunic, then calmly walked to the edge of the gorge.

At this point the old man stopped speaking as the methodic blipping of the monitor turned to a shrill buzz. Another machine tripped into a piercing alarm as several masked nurses rushed into the ward along with an orderly pushing a crash cart. The old man made no further sound at all.

Amid the commotion, I quickly fell asleep.

How Did the World Sound?

Judith Barkley

How did the world sound
before leaf blowers and weed whackers,
before chain saws, power mowers,
and the arching whine
of garbage-truck forklifts?

It was the swirl of winter wind,
a hum through leafless oaks,
as I skated Indian Creek,
my blades slicing ice,
a white shawl of snow
falling silently on my shoulders.
Or on a spring day, in a field nearby,
the cows' velvet lowing.
Or a whirring so delicate—
a hummingbird—
when I came too close
to her tiny nest
sculpted between two twigs
of the Australian Boxwood.

On occasion, I like to hear
the coyotes' yelps as they navigate
the canyon near my home.
Too, I think, once in this life,
I would like to hear the wail
of wolves in the wild, raw.

Yet, perhaps, it is enough
to contemplate the puzzle
of my cat's purr—
the ebb and flow of blood,
the vibration between larynx and diaphragm.
One foreleg and paw across my arm,
she lays her head on my shoulder
and sings her mystery to me.
I stroke her head and listen to her sound—
deep throated, soft.

A Midnight Conversation

Judy Reeves

"*I* know it's late but…"

"Never mind," he says. "I'll take the phone outside."

He says he wants to watch the Pleiades change shape, the way those girls lift their skirts as the night goes on, rising at midnight on the eastern horizon and creeping higher and higher through the night until by four a.m. they are directly overhead.

He talks about the sunflowers and how, by August, they've grown nearly to the balcony where he'll sleep tonight, their big yellow faces nodding as he talks about the fish he caught in the river that day and how its rainbow skin captured the light and how cold the water was around his legs and what it did to his balls. He speaks of the blackberries he put in his canteen.

"Yes, I still have a canteen," he says, "from Boy Scouts." And he tells you how a good canteen is better than a plastic thermos for keeping blackberries cold and how, in August, when you walk along the river, stone to stone, and lean out to where the berries drag the water, you can see the bottom of the river and that poems can be found there. "Like the blackberries," he says, "you just have to know where to look."

He sways in his hammock on the midnight porch and you, with your eyes closed, imagining. Over the phone, you hear a train in the distance and he says, "Listen for the whistle." There are rules against sounding the whistle after eleven o'clock, but there's one engineer, Old Tom, who can't resist.

"Old Tom used to have a lover in town," he says, "and he blows his whistle just to remind her what she's missing."

Ficus Tree

Judy Hansen

you were the first thing we saw when we arrived at the house.
our eyes climbed your muscular trunk that narrowed then reached
wide, limbs dense with leaves, towering over buena vista avenue.

wild and sprawling, home to busy sparrows we saw only when
they darted in or out, and what shade and breeze beneath. we
looked up a full ten minutes before we explored the house we later
decided to buy.

we looked up and smiled at you, such a beast of a tree, over one
hundred years old, we came to learn. and later we talked about the
house with "the tree" as if it were an asset like a swimming pool or
tennis court, on which we based our final decision to buy.

two years later, when the workers came to lace and trim you back,
you stood there stoically. the arborist scaled your branches in a
cherry picker with chain saw or pole pruner in hand. he and his
two-man crew blocked the street with orange cones as if it were

an emergency procedure. from our porch we watched morning
doves fly back and forth in alarm, spreading the word of
destruction. your solid trunk remained still, as your limbs fell
around you in a giant heap of fresh leaves ground into mulch there
on the spot, up through a funnel to the big white truck parked
in front.

you held your ground. observant, watchful. we see through you
now to the ocean. we see over you to the reservoir. your crown is
bare but undaunted.

I depend on your constancy standing there, watchful, as I leave for
work in the morning, and still the first thing I see arriving home in
the evening, when your western back drop is a pale orange, your
grey limbs silhouetted against the sky.

A Little South of Canas, on Route 20

William Cass

My wife, Sarah, and I were traveling through the western portion of the Swan River Valley in Montana on our way back to Seattle from Havre, where we had been to the wedding of her cousin, Lauren. The wedding had been nice. Like Sarah and me, Lauren and her husband, Nick, had waited until their midthirties to marry. We'd spent at least part of every summer for years together at a lake in Idaho and were close. The two of them had met in Missoula in college and had lived together afterwards there for fifteen years, where they both worked as nurses. Then Nick's mother died and, a few months later, his father passed away as well. They decided to go in with Nick's brothers and take over the family ranch outside of Havre. They wanted to continue to grow wheat and graze sheep, but Nick also wanted to try raising llamas as pack animals. Lauren's own mother, down in Helena, was aging quickly as well and wanted to see them make things official.

So, their plan made sense. Of course, it also put to rest the ideas we'd kicked around together, dreams of getting out of the rat race, the four of us starting a Christmas tree farm, or something like that. Now Sarah and I were clearly on our own as far as anything along those lines was concerned.

Their ceremony was simple and lighthearted: appropriate for Lauren and Nick. They seemed very happy. After the wedding, there was a brief reception at a country-western bar that had a big open-air patio in the back, and everyone square-danced. That was a lot of fun. It had been an early-afternoon wedding, and before the sun had set, the newlyweds were on the train heading for a canoe-trip honeymoon in the Boundary Waters along the Minnesota and Canadian border.

The rest of the wedding party all spent the night at an old scout camp that a boyhood friend of Nick's had bought outside town on a reservoir. Sarah and I snuck off with a bottle of wine, went skinny-dipping, and built a campfire under a canopy of stars that looked about as full and dense as you could possibly imagine. We slept out on a sandy shore and zipped our sleeping bags together. We lay on our backs, looked up, and didn't say anything for a long time.

Finally, Sarah whispered, "My."

As quietly as I could, I said, "Exactly."

The next morning was a Sunday. Late September in Northern Montana and about as good as it gets: full fall shuffling in the wings, still sun-splashed, the light clean and white, gently warm at full day and faint-whisper shadows later on. We'd taken a couple days of personal leave from our teaching jobs and planned a slow trip back with no particular agenda, except to check out a few areas we'd heard about that we thought might be good for potential bed-and-breakfast sites.

I thought about the night Nick and Lauren called with their news. It was winter and another dark, long evening of rain. We offered our congratulations, of course. Circumstances, after all, had just presented themselves. But later that night, a few hours before dawn, I awoke to find Sarah leaning against our bedroom window looking out at the rain. I sat up, cleared my throat. She didn't turn around, but just said, "We still have to look, Sam. I'm tired of this city and this so-called life. I want to start a family. Our chances are slipping by. We can do it alone."

So that Sunday after the wedding, we headed west along Route 2, then slowly south out of Glacier National Park along the eastern shore of Flathead Lake. We had the road pretty much to ourselves. The mountains rose up to our left, gray and scraggly, the clear Little Bitterroot River to our right was shallow and tumbled over round, brown rocks. It played hide and seek through meadows, cottonwoods beginning to turn, and stands of pines. Occasionally a flat, green, still pond spread itself out on one side of the road or the other.

It was a beautiful stretch of country and an interesting one from a practical standpoint, as well. Bigfork on Flathead Lake was less than an hour away to the north and had a popular summer theater season. The Whitefish Ski Area was only slightly further to the north. The Chamber of Commerce in Lonepine, the tiny town in the center of the valley, had sent us some literature, and it appeared that the schools were reputable and our credentials reciprocal, the winters comparatively mild, and real estate still reasonably priced. So, we looked intently as we motored along.

We studied pictures of property in the windows of a few real estate offices that were closed on Sunday afternoon. Then, just south of Canas, we drove by a hand-painted sign tacked to a tree by the side of the road that said: "10 acres for sale and house. Riverfront. By owner." An arrow was drawn next to the address.

I pulled over to the side of the road and looked at Sarah. She said, "Why not?"

She scribbled the pertinent information on the back of an envelope, and we started down a long gravel drive that ended in a wide patch of short green grass. A small barn sat on one side of the yard; next to it, a split-rail corral with two brown horses and, beyond that, the Swan River. The river formed a horseshoe around the property until it disappeared into octaves of cattails, cottonwoods, pines, and gray mountains in the distance.

On the other side of the yard stood a large white farmhouse with a porch on three sides and a screened balcony surrounding the second floor. Big clay pots of yellow and purple pansies perched on the steps leading up to the front door, and other flowers and shrubs nestled themselves in neat beds in front. Surrounding the house itself, grass gave way to meadow with a couple of outbuildings off to one side.

We sat in the car for a long moment without speaking. I could hear the river running fast. One of the horses snorted and swished its tail; the other shook its head. Besides that, it was still; no noise from the highway.

Finally, I said, "I like it."

Sarah was nodding slowly. "I'll bet there are huckleberries in season all over," she said and opened her door.

I followed her towards the front of the house. A high woman's voice stopped us from the second floor balcony. I could only see her vague figure through the screen. In a thick dialect she said, "Yoo-hoo, hello! Welcome!"

Sarah said, "We saw your sign. We hope it's all right."

"Yes, is all right! Wait for moment. I'm be right down."

"Is she Hungarian?" Sarah whispered.

"I don't know. She's something. She sounds lively."

Then she was out the front door: a short, stooped, gray-haired woman wearing a beige cardigan sweater buttoned to the neck, a white apron, blue stretch pants, and fleece-lined slippers. She clapped her hands and put her head back smiling.

Sarah repeated, "We saw your sign."

"Yes," the woman said. "I'm Gretchen. Bill is out. He will be back soon. He's gone to Polson. He is the one who talks with the people who are interest in the property, but if you like to look around, is all right. He should return soon. The trail down the river is marked with little red ribbons; he cleared it only this week. It think is good, cleared, yes. You walk and look if you like, then come back and I show you our house. I put coffee on. Look."

"All right," I said.

"Look," she said making a shooing gesture. "Look to your heart's pleasure."

She went back into the house holding her apron. We smiled and shrugged at each another, then started across the meadow and onto the trail marked with ribbon. When we were gone from the house a ways, Sarah giggled and said, "I guess we're supposed to look."

I said, "Seems so."

Big white pillows of clouds clustered against the crest of the Swan Range. The dark granite peaks looked like rude scratches against the late afternoon sky, whose blue had deepened. The valley itself fell off to the east beyond the river. Scattered patches of reddening huckleberry bushes clung among swatches of late fireweed and St. John's wart that colored the meadow on either side of the path. Sarah stopped to point at a deer that stood still at the far end of the meadow. Its wide eyes stared at us until it bounded off suddenly into the trees. Sarah turned and grinned at me, her eyes as wide as the deer's.

After perhaps a hundred yards, a cool breath wafted over us, and we came through the brush hard against the river. The trail fell off a short cliff of red-brown earth. The commotion we made scared an osprey off its nest at the top of a lightning-charred fir and we watched it call as it flew off over the treetops.

We stood and watched the river. The sun was still on it, speckled like the trout I was certain sat in the shadows against its far bank, the river there calico colored and rippled. A soft breeze tossed the undersides of the cottonwood leaves spinning like sequins and the boughs of the pines dipped, it seemed, grudgingly.

I heard Sarah say, "We could make pies. Ben and I."

"Ben's not born yet."

"You and I, then. After you get home from school. And afterwards, Ben or Claire or whatever we name them could help. We'd serve our guests pie for breakfast. It would be something to tell their friends back in Nob Hill or Medina or Lake Oswego. They'd say, 'And we had pie for breakfast.' They'd say it happily and I'd be happy to prepare it for them."

I said, "You make good pie."

Sarah tossed a branch into the river. It bounced downstream on the current, then spun left against a deep pool under an uprooted tree trunk.

"This reminds me of where we used to fish when we lived in Alaska," Sarah said. "Back when we did things like that. Back when we still had our senses."

I nodded slowly, but she didn't see. We turned and returned along the trail without talking. We walked without haste on the soft earth and pine needles. When we came up to the house, we knocked, and Sarah took my hand and squeezed it. Gretchen came to the door smelling of cheap perfume. She had changed into a blue linen dress and sandals, but still wore the same cardigan and apron.

"You like the river?" she asked opening the door for us. "Is so beautiful."

Sarah said, "We like it very much."

"Now, our home," Gretchen said. "I don't know where is Bill. He's back soon, though. Come."

She led us into a front room with wide, sun-washed floorboards, a big fireplace made from round river rocks, denim-covered couch and chairs, and linen curtains stirring on the small breeze. Sarah glanced at me happily, and I knew that there was no real need to look further. But we let Gretchen show us through the rest of the big house. It was a wonderful place. She told us that her husband had built it after a model of a Dutch farmhouse, and the careful craftsmanship was obvious from the start. She paused in each room and admired it with her hands held in front of her and a small, almost straight line of smile on her lips.

"Bill set off to build this house thirty years ago and is still building," she told us. "Is never stop building."

We went through the living room, dining room, kitchen, and upstairs to a separate wing that they had built for family guests. Each room opened onto the screened balcony that was decorated with cushioned furniture that Bill had crafted by hand from fallen pines on the property. It was sad, she said, that so few relatives had come, but they were all far away in California. Except for a sort of den that she used for sewing, the rooms upstairs sat empty and unused.

Gretchen started down some back stairs and Sarah stopped me with a hand on my arm. She whispered, "Pinch me."

I nodded.

We followed Gretchen downstairs and came to two bedrooms behind the main living area. One, filled with old photographs, was clearly their own. A hooked rug lay on the floor by a four-poster bed covered with a chenille bedspread. The door to the other bedroom was closed. Gretchen knocked quietly, then led us inside. A man about our age lay on his side in green paisley pajamas on a medical supply bed around which a protective bar was raised. The man's mouth broke into a smile and his tongue lolled over his bottom lip. His disheveled hair covered part of one eye, and his head was lopsided a bit, flatter than it should have been in back and peaking abruptly on top. A cartoon played on a small television that sat on a tray table next to the bed; bottles of pills were arranged in a row next to the television. A wheelchair stood at the foot of the bed with a package of adult diapers on the seat.

Gretchen walked over to him and wiped the drool off his chin and pillow with a bandana that was draped over the bar. Then she kissed him on the forehead and held his hand.

She turned to us and said happily, "This is Robert. Our son."

I nodded. Sarah said hello. A clock chimed somewhere in the house, an old clock, I imagined, that either I hadn't seen or hadn't noticed.

"This room has own bathroom," Gretchen said pointing. "Bill build special supports in tub, but can be removed. Easy. Is nothing to remove."

Sarah stepped forward and put her hand on Robert's shoulder. "You have a lovely home," she said quietly.

I looked around the room. It was covered with crude watercolor paintings, of what, I wasn't sure. There were two pieces of white corkboard propped up on the bureau, which seemed to be unfinished collections of mounted butterflies and fall leaves. A fishing pole stood in the corner, a simple bamboo rod with a line and bobber, but no reel.

I hadn't seen one like it since I was a child. A photograph sat tilted on the wall: Robert at around his present age and a man considerably older than Gretchen with a small, kind smile and downturned eyes; they were in the yard holding what appeared to be jars of cloudy honey.

Gretchen followed my gaze and said, "These are Robert's things. He finds things with Bill. They keep bees. They do things. They go off together."

I nodded some more. The air was close in the room and smelled slightly of camphor. Robert sighed and made a soft clicking sound.

"Is too early for supper," Gretchen told him. She kissed him again and smoothed his hair. "I come back soon."

She led us out of the room and gently closed the door. We followed her down the hall and into the kitchen. We sat down at the table, which she had set with bone china and a percolator that bubbled on a hot pad. I looked at the county-fair award certificates she'd received for her quilts and jams that hung in plain black frames on the wall. The light had fallen outside and long shadows stretched across the room. Dust floated in the shafts of sunlight that angled through the windows.

Gretchen poured us all coffee and unrolled blueprints to which I had difficulty paying proper attention. She told us of how particular Bill had been in his construction, how he'd included extra insulation, how he'd vented the fireplace to help heat the house and had carried the rocks up himself from the river for the hearth, about the deep closets and double-paned windows. These were things about which I needed no clarification. From the somber look on Sarah's face, neither did she. We stirred our coffee, and every now and then one of us sipped it.

When Gretchen had finished, Sarah let her set out a plate of gingersnaps before she asked, "Why are you moving?"

Gretchen nodded and looked out the window towards the river. "Bill is good man. He retire from highway department many years ago. He save careful." She sighed. "But is worried about his health, his age. Is worried about us. Is thinking we should move back to California near family, near hospital, doctors."

They looked at each other. Gretchen shrugged. "Is good plan. He thinks maybe we can buy mobile home in court down there. Still put little money in bank for rainy days. Family nearby. Is good plan."

We watched her look outside again. She nodded. More quietly, she said, "Make sense."

I wondered how many thousands of times she'd stared out that window. We followed her gaze. I could hear the river, but couldn't see it. The sound of the cartoon from the television in the bedroom was also audible. Gretchen's hand trembled a bit on the teacup, rattling it faintly against the saucer. Sarah reached over and set her own hand gently on the older woman's, steadying it. Gretchen turned back to her and gave her a small smile. We sat like that for a long moment until Sarah finally stood up and said that we should be going. Gretchen nodded and walked us out to the car.

In the dim light, she said, "All right, then."

She opened her arms and Sarah hugged her. I walked around to the driver's side. As I got in, they were still holding each other. I started the engine.

In a small voice, I heard Gretchen say, "I'm sorry. I never show you the bees."

I watched a thin ground fog creep across the meadow behind the barn. For several long moments, it was quiet. Then I heard Sarah say, "You know you can't leave. You mustn't."

I heard Gretchen say sadly, "I don't know where is Bill."

"He'll come home," Sarah told her. "Then everything will be fine."

One of them sighed; I thought it was Gretchen, but I wasn't sure. Finally, Sarah climbed inside and closed the door. I didn't study things as we drove away; I didn't want to. Perhaps Gretchen waved, perhaps she just stood there, perhaps she was crying, perhaps she walked back to the house. I'll never know.

We headed down Route 20 towards Plains. The road was straight and traffic was all but nonexistent. I looked over at Sarah once, but her head was turned towards her window. At Hot Springs, I switched on the headlights. At Plains, I turned the radio on low to a classical station I found somehow on the FM out of Billings, and we turned west on Route 200 along the Clark Fork.

At some point, Sarah said distinctly, "We'll send a card."

But I didn't reply. We drove for long time without speaking a word. I didn't ask Sarah where she wanted to stop next or if she was hungry; I just drove. We made it a little past the Idaho border before I pulled off the highway at a cinder block hotel next to a diner whose white light in the semi-darkness suggested it might still be open.

I got us a room and we carried our things inside. Sarah said she wanted to take a bath, and I said I'd go down and get us something to eat. I turned the television on before I left, though we rarely watched it at home. Maybe I just wanted some noise. I'm not sure.

I wasn't very hungry, and I guessed Sarah wasn't either. I bought a plastic container of fruit salad and stopped outside our room before going inside. Just the slightest hint of daylight still dwindled on the horizon, purple-blue. Stars were out again, and I wondered if there could be any skies anywhere as big as the ones in that part of the West during that season of the year. As big and as full. As still and as quiet. As lovely.

When I got back inside, Sarah was already in bed with the covers pulled up to her chin. No lights were on, just the flicker from the television. I got in bed beside her and put the carton with a couple of plastic forks between us. Neither of us ate much. We just nibbled and looked at some situation comedy on the TV. After a while, I carried the trash into the bathroom and threw it away. When

I came back out, Sarah was turned away from me, the television still and dark.

We lay in bed listening, I suppose, to the crickets in the high reeds outside the hotel or the occasional murmur of traffic up the road on the highway. We lay still there in the relative quiet, as we had the night before. We were a little better than an hour from Spokane; then it was four more back to Seattle, where I supposed I would go into school the next afternoon to do some lesson planning.

Perhaps it was Sarah who first rolled over and held me, or perhaps I made one of my small, hopeful gestures: a finger rubbing a hip, a small brush of hair behind an ear, a tiny kiss on a shoulder. Time passed and I can't truly remember. I do know that after holding one another for a long time, Sarah whispered, "Don't ever leave me," that then I squeezed her, and that afterwards, we both slept.

Cats & Laughter

Martha Kinkade

When I was five, I could grab chicken heads
quicker than the blade could chop them off.
The heads and claws I'd hold in my apron,
stand in the center of the barnyard surrounded
by cats and toss my givings. I loved the cat hisses
and savored the last head just for the runt.

Just before our junior high soiree, Bryan
picked up a hot wire. I imagined his legs
shooting off like bottle rockets. In a borrowed
dress, I danced with Bryan in his wheelchair.
The kids called us—two mad badgers. Shortly
after, they went back to calling him the all
too familiar: drool hound, pimple lips.

At our high school reunion, while we watched
the couples jitterbug, Bryan asked me to tell
my cat story—one more time. Perhaps we laughed.
Perhaps we didn't. We stared somewhat blank
into the dance floor. He was in prosthetics
and I suffered—a Cat Queen sensibility.

Critical Mass

Judy Reeves

She stood on the corner reading the blinking sign: wait wait wait, on and off, in red diodesian letters. She was on her way to the liquor store at the corner, pick up a shorty, then on to the Humane Society to pet the dogs.

It was her regular Wednesday routine—up early, get the laundry out of the way. Wednesdays being her assigned day for the communal washer and dryer in the basement of her apartment building. Eight apartments—seven days. She volunteered to share Wednesdays with Butch. Neither of them had much laundry to do since the downsizing. They shared the cost of the detergent, too. The bleach and dryer flyers—that's what Butch called them—those flimsy papers that she insisted on using to get the static from her underpants. Nothing worse than blue sparks shooting from your you- know-what, she said.

Wednesdays, two to five p.m., the Humane Society opened the pens to people who wanted to spend time with the dogs, but couldn't adopt a pet of their own—whatever reason, mostly space. For her, it was the downsizing.

She used to have a dog, little cocker named Curly, but he got run over by a bicycle. A whole bunch of bicycles, really. One of those Friday night Critical Mass rides. Maybe more than two hundred of them, cranking down 30th in a huge, rabble-rousing pack. Poor Curly—one after another of those bikers running over him. She can't even bear to think of it anymore, what was left of him after the last of the bikers passed.

That's when she started buying shorties in the morning, and it was after that she was downsized.

The light turned green. She crossed, bought her beer, and set off for Sherman Street. She wanted to be first in line at the Pound. The Pound. She slipped every now and then, called the place by its old name: The Dog Pound. Couldn't for the life of her remember when they changed the name to Humane Society, as if what they did to the dogs no one wanted was any different.

She popped open the can, took a long gulp.

Today, she thought, she'd climb in the pen with the shepherds. Those big, sturdy dogs could stand up to a rowdy rub behind the ears, a tight hug around the neck, and most didn't mind when you leaned right into their chests and cried as much as you needed.

Shopping

Elizabeth Trude

We sat in Sbarro's, beneath unflattering lights,
the rushing hush and quiet clamor of the mall
dulled by the hum of ovens,
the shuffling of paper plates.
He set the bag beside himself,
I took the seat across.

Two sodas sat on the table
between us, he lifted his,
took a long pull and announced:
"I have to use the bathroom,"
I politely smiled and watched him go.

Then I did it.
I could say I did it because I was young—
but I wasn't that young. Not really.

I watched the door swing shut behind him,
made my move.
I *grabbed* for his cup and swiftly brought
the straw to my mouth…

hesitated…

then placed it between my lips,
imagining that the unknown warmth of his mouth lingered,
and immediately, I began to tremble,
quiver—senseless.

The arches of my feet felt it first,
then an ebb and flow, giving and pulling until
I came to,
white knuckling the plastic cup,
straw clenched and bent between my teeth.

Pushing the soda away from me back onto the table,
the men's room door swung open.
He sat lightly, innocently lifting the scarf from the bag,

"Do you think she'll like it?"
"What? Oh, yes…yes. Of course! Your wife will love it."

Doesn't Mean Anything

Scott Barbour

We're getting drunk on the skanky yellow couch in Julie's basement. Again. Me and Andrew and Julie and Renee. And Renee goes let's play truth or dare, and we're all what are we, twelve? But she goes come on you guys, it'll be fun. So we end up hearing how Julie wants to do this guy called Sean AKA Mr. Lacrosse, and I'm looking for a window to jump out but all I can find is the little slit above the water heater that's only big enough for the cat.

So then it's my turn and I pick *dare* because I suck at lying. Renee gets this grin on one side of her face like she thinks she's the spawn of Satan. She even has dyed black hair and black lipstick and painted black fingernails for the full spawn-of-Satan ensemble. She points at me. She points at Andrew. Then she says, one minute. With tongues.

Me and Andrew keep saying no fuckin' way but Julie and Renee are all everyone does it, it doesn't mean anything, and it's true. Every week there's rumors about different guys making out, even popular eleventh graders with hot girlfriends and no one thinks they're gay. It's like it makes them even cooler.

Me and Andrew look at each other, but we've been drinking punch mixed with rum that Julie stole from her mom so everything's whooshing like the couch is a boat going down a river with huge rapids and Niagara Falls at the end. Andrew's black hair sticks straight up on one side like he just got attacked by a bear that got him drunk first.

Even though we're drunk or maybe because we're drunk, we're both smiling like we just did something really stupid in front of the whole school and what can you do at a time like that but smile? I'm all, are we really gonna do this? And Andrew goes holy fuckin' shit. And we scoot closer with one leg up on the couch and don't ask me why but my heart's going about ten million miles an hour. Then our faces get really close but we start laughing and pull them apart again. Then we zoom in and I can see his pores and smell his booze breath. And then our noses and lips touch but we start laughing and back away and Renee says one minute. With tongues.

So then we start again and Renee and Julie are hooting and I'm laughing even though my lips are on Andrew's. I'm like there's no way this is happening, this is not happening, but it's happening. Renee says forty more seconds, and then she goes with tongues, so we start sliding our tongues together while trying not to laugh and I'm thinking, I'm tongue-kissing my best friend, how wrong is that? But then the music stops. Everything gets quiet, and all I can hear is Andrew and me breathing through our noses, and our mouths smacking, and we're not laughing anymore.

After our one minute ended, Andrew cranked the Metallica and bumped his shoulder against different walls, even though they were cinder block. I started guzzling rum punch until I puked on the dog's blanket, and when I got home my parents knew I was drunk and grounded me for five years.

At school on Monday me and Andrew tried to act like it was no big deal, but soon the rumor was all over school, and it didn't make us cooler because we weren't popular eleventh graders with hot girlfriends, we were virgin freshmen and everyone knew it and now probably gay, too. At lunch time after we ate, me and Andrew both just sat there waiting for the bell, looking everywhere but at each other. It was like, *ring already,* you stupid fucking bell.

Intervals

Jennifer Simpson

One leg stands on
solid ground, the other
tapping, searching
for the next
foothold, feeling
naught but air—

In between now
and tomorrow, I am
unsettled, my breath
shallow.

Yes, it was
a deliberate choice to insert that   space there
for it is in the space

between breaths   that change occurs.

℘hantom

Eber Lambert

*I*often remember sitting in my father's severed lap, my bare feet dangling off the front of his wheelchair, my hands clutching his green khaki pant legs tied into fat knots where his thighs ended. He called me Phantom. In 1971 we lived in North Charleston, in subsidized subsistence, in a black-and-white, Cronkite-evening-news kind of the world with our spotty reception and horizontal-hold problems. Nothing a good smack couldn't fix. My Mom lived in a crooked picture frame hung on the front room wall, a graduation-picture smile behind finger-smudged glass, surrounded by fading whisky stains splattered from a thrown tumbler that once shattered a few inches away. I heard her voice on the phone sometimes. She seemed nice enough.

A few times a week, Dad would roll with his buddies down to the VA to play cards in the afternoon and drink their way back home after dark. On weekdays I'd walk home from school with some big kids that were allowed to cross the state road. Then I'd crawl into the house through the skinny cellar window in the back. The dark cellar smelled like dried swamp mud and was full of cobwebs. I was the only one who ever went down there but only for the twelve seconds it took to get from the window to the top of the steps.

Most afternoons I would eat saltines with mayonnaise and watch Opie, Jethro, and Gilligan on channel five. When Dad got home, we would open a can of something from a box of PX groceries that some nice ladies would leave on our porch every other week. Sometimes Dad fell asleep before the food was hot and I would get to eat the whole can all by myself. I'd cover him with the afghan and go to bed whenever I felt like it.

One Saturday morning, before cartoons were even over, Dad in a rare cheerful mood rolled down the hall and said, "Come on Phantom, we're going for a ride!" I held open the front door then hopped on and sat between his knotted pant legs, as we sped off down the sidewalk. My Dad laughed when I made screeching tire sounds when we took turns or when I squealed when he popped a wheelie. He rolled us all the way down to Sumner Avenue where we sat and watch the Fourth of July parade. People moved out of the way and let us roll right up to the front by the curb. I waved a little flag an old man in a baggy uniform was handing out, watched pretty girls twirling batons and drummers fooling around but not missing a beat. I saw my Dad cry for the only time ever. And I accidentally let go of my balloon. It was a big one, perfectly clear with a smaller balloon inside made to look like a globe of the earth floating in space. I squinted real hard as I watched that little world trapped inside that balloon sail up into the humid Carolina haze, staring up into the sky until I couldn't see it anymore. Dad said it would eventually lose its helium and float back down somewhere far away. I remember wondering how long that would take and where would it land when it did.

Today I'm on a side street in Lower Manhattan near Battery Park, among a cluster of other struggling artists and functional junkies, hustling my pencil sketches and some acrylics that I paint in a shithole apartment in South Bronx. I've been living alone for twenty-odd years, save a couple of women that have come, grown tired of me, then moved on. I'm standing here smoking a Camel and periodically sipping cheap whisky from a flask. A legless vet wearing an Iraq war camo jacket rolls by in a wheelchair. It's a hot and humid summer day and I occasionally catch myself looking up into the sky.

Bloomies

Regina Morin

Walking into Bloomingdale's
on a brisk February afternoon,
the wind from the bay pushing
against my neck, the icy column
of the chrome handle on the glass door
pouring a chill into my palm,
I am embraced by the
deliciousness of things:
a lavender silk tie against
the mannequin's still shirt;
the rounded jewels of creams
that soothe the skin; the upright
towers of absolute light
inside a perfume vial.
And always, lurking outside
my vision, the delicious
muffin-maids of commerce,
so polished in their black,
crisp suits, their hands outstretched
for the offering I bring: a slim
credit card with nothing more
than mere magnetism at its heel.

the last king of sanity

Jackson Crow-Mickle

he sits in a beat-up fold out
smoking from the stepped-on pack
he found behind the five-and-dime.
his feet loll out in front of him,
mismatched shoes over matching socks.
he takes a long, slow pull
from his bagged forty,
cracked teeth mocking those passing
by, in their cars.
every time the light turns red
there is a new voice to curse him,
condemn him for a lay about.
he laughs when they prove him right,
tapping his cardboard indulgently—
if the world ended today,
i'd die happier than any of You.

Smoke

John Farrell MacDonald

*T*he scent of smoke fits with the painting until I stop to think about it. I hear no alarm, and no one's nearby to ask, "Do you smell smoke?" The hallway is dimly lit and I don't see anything that might be its source, so I head off to warn the museum staff.

I move quickly without actually running and find a security guard near the elevator. "Excuse me, sir," I say, "I don't want to cause undue concern, but I seem to be smelling smoke down one of the hallways."

He looks at me with his stiffly rumpled face and black eyes. I take it as umbrage. After the incident with George, I'm not so sure of myself. I, a tentative and fidgety fabulist, have just brought the guard trouble.

His eyes narrow and his hand moves slowly to the walkie-talkie on his belt while he asks, "Where?"

"Down the little, dark hall off the north wing. I'll show you."

His eyebrows raise and he begins to move, motioning me to lead the way. He speaks to his radio as he walks, "I have a report of a possible fire on 3 north. A visitor is smelling smoke." The radio squawks back and he responds, "Yes, yes. I'm checking it out."

"Let's go," he says, urging me to pick up the pace.

By the time the guard and a harried-looking facility man finish assessing the situation, a small crowd has gathered to see what the commotion is about. But there's no evidence of any smoke or fire.

"Everyone, there's no problem," the guard announces. "Please continue to enjoy your visit. Everything is fine. No need for alarm."

I catch the word "fire" in the group's subdued chatter, but they disperse after watching the facility man saunter back to work.

The guard, arms crossed, looks at me with his hard face only a little softer and says, "Maybe you just got carried away with the painting. We get that sometimes. Maybe you should take a break, wander down to the gift shop, get some coffee, relax a bit before you continue your visit."

His eyes move toward the exit with expectation. He's not just making a polite suggestion. I take one more look at the painting before I go: Smoke rising from a campfire in a forest of Aspens, a hint of rustle in their leaves. Pony standing nearby with an Indian blanket on its back and a tightly woven basket at its side.

A coffee, perhaps a mocha with whip, suddenly sounds good.

I'm on my usual bus home when a kid with a dirty grey backpack stops in the aisle next to me. It looks like he wants the empty seat by the window, but instead he just says my name. My full name. "Mr. James Cagney Siva?" he asks.

The bespectacled punk—maybe a sophomore—couldn't look more bored. Anywhere near campus, I'm not surprised to be recognized by someone I don't know, but usually she would be a girl who'd say, "Hello Professor Siva," even though I'm not a full professor. Then I'd smile, ask if she's in one of my classes, while pretending to be aloof and uncaring. But the "Mr." and "Cagney" bit has me all off, and I just mutter, "Yes?"

"You've been served," he says and stuffs an envelope in front of me with his free hand. I take it and the kid continues to the back of the bus.

A buzz in my gut tells me what it's about, but I'm going to wait until I get home to open it. I stash it in my satchel.

I lay the contents of the envelope on the kitchen table next to a pile of unopened mail: two letters and a check. One letter, bearing the stamp of the San Diego County Superior Court, is a restraining order, requiring me to stay at least 500 feet away from both George Stanwood Ellison and the San Diego State University Campus for the next five years. The second, under SDSU Department of American Indian Studies letterhead, is from old George himself, department chair, notifying me that my position as Adjunct Assistant Professor has been terminated effective immediately. The check covers my pay to date and for the next sixty days. Added all up, the amount isn't half bad, even considering the horrendous chunk of tax withheld.

Though I'm not too surprised, the letters have me shaking, standing there at the table while I reread them. I sit to gather my thoughts.

The relic that started it all catches my eye, sitting there on the kitchen windowsill. It gives me a defiant glare, taunting me. The tusk—that's what I believe the relic to be—stands about a foot high and is intricately carved. I found it on an expedition with old George in the Anza-Borrego desert, and I'm quite sure that he has its companion. Just looking at it, I could tell it was one of a matched set. Only George knew where I found it. Only George could have known where to find its mate. I couldn't let him get away with it and, well, I guess I got a little heated.

Next day I'm not over the shakes, so I take the bus down to the museum. Rumple Face is there. He lets me be and I spend a good hour in front of the painting.

I swear I can still smell smoke.

For some reason the painting seems different than what I remember. Something subtle, maybe the lighting or the direction of sunlight.

I go back to the museum every day for the next week, except for Monday when it's closed. The smell of smoke persists and each day I notice subtle changes. Day turning to evening, a slight shift in the wind.

Wednesday is late night at the museum and, though I arrive at ten in the morning when the doors open, I'm prepared to stay until closing at midnight. I am determined to watch the painting, to catch it changing.

Ever-present Rumple Face is patient but keeps an eye on me, only objecting to the sack lunch I'd brought for the stay. "No food in the museum," he says. I dump it and decide a day without food won't hurt me any.

By eleven p.m. the only change I've noticed is in the pony's stance. Her weight has shifted and her front left leg has moved just a bit forward. I record this in my moleskin notebook when Rumple Face comes in, saying, "Hey, buddy. Why don't you go home and get some sleep. It's almost tomorrow."

Sitting on the bench in front of the painting, I turn and say, "Sure, sure. I'll go in a bit," and I watch him go as he resumes his rounds.

Back to the painting, only an hour left, I focus. When the museum lights dim before closing, I expect Rumple Face will appear to usher me out. Until then, I ignore everything but the painting.

I'm not sure how long before I sense a change around me. Except for the rustling of the Aspen leaves, and the flicker of the fire, it's quiet. I'm at peace, enjoying the breeze, grasping every moment of the evening dusk.

The pony raises her head, startled by a movement behind me. It must be Rumple Face, already. I'm not about to acknowledge his presence. I sit rigid and waiting.

The touch on my shoulder is gentler than expected. I turn, but it's not Rumple Face. A young native girl, dressed in a leather, stands there smiling. She says something I understand to mean "please follow."

I rise and walk with her into the forest.

Pale Blonde With Sadness

Karen Stromberg

See, behind her eyes
moving beneath her skin
the hushed green of old summers,
faded faces, still hung with thorns—
they rise like the drowned in warming water.
And see, in her opened hand, a curled memory,
an anniversary which neither dims nor dies.
Know this, the courage she once couldn't find
still lives, a phalange of anger.
Let her be. She stands by a window.
It is dusk again,
  or dawn.

The Silver Twinkie

Nancy Klann

It'd been three decades since I last saw Yvonne Carter, and never would I have made the drive if she hadn't needed me.

After five hours, the highway became less and less congested, until mine was the lone car on the isolated road. The Mojave Desert scenery stretched for miles and seemed unforgiving. Yucca and barrel cactus rippled through ponds of distant vapors, like caution signs. I believe the tour books call it desolate grandeur, but it seemed more like windswept insanity.

Yvonne and I were best friends during the roller-skating years. We were laugh-til-you-blow-milk-out-of-your-nose friends, from third grade until the summer before high school, when the Carters abruptly moved. We promised to stay close but, as those things go, we lost touch.

After the initial excitement of hearing from her, I asked how she found me.

"On the Internet," she said. "I use the library computers for free." Her voice hissed over a poor connection. "It was easy. I plunked in a couple of matter-of-facts, and I'll be damned if your name and address didn't come up on the screen."

"I'm so glad you did."

"Fancy-schmancy you," she said, "living in Beverly Hills."

"On the outskirts." I laughed. "How about you?"

"I'm in the desert," she said. "God, I've missed you over the years, Rosy."

"I've missed you, too," I said, uncomfortable with my fib.

"Whenever I'm feeling unhinged, I look at the photo of us at Magic Mountain, and somehow it helps me. Remember how much fun we had that day?"

"Well, sure." I said. But I didn't really□ not the way she did. She recited word-for-word conversations, and then recounted other trips we'd taken. Exact details about what we wore, and how the mustard from the corn dogs dripped down our arms. I grew self-conscious about my memory. It was as though a giant blotter expunged all the details of our friendship. Even so, some of the things she said simply couldn't have happened. Or maybe they could have.

Yvonne sounded a bit wacky and, yes, that part I remembered well. Soon, just like when we were kids, she made me laugh. We grew nostalgic over tap dance lessons, two-handed canasta games during summer break, and listening to the Top 40 Countdown together. Our conversation glided smooth as a waltz, with Yvonne taking the lead and filling in all the particulars.

"Remember how you'd bail me out of trouble?" she said. "How you could rationalize to the teachers, until nothing we did was our fault?"

I was flattered. I think.

"Are you still loyal to the bone, Rosy? Still polite as punch? Still perfect as a china doll? Can you still talk your way out of anything?"

"Yvonne, stop it." I feared the teasing could turn mean, even though her voice remained airy.

"Okay, Okay, but God, I'd love to see you again. I'd drive to your place in a heartbeat, but my car's on the blink."

"Is it serious?"

"I like to say it bit the dust."

"What?"

"Like I said, I'm out here in the desert, and somehow sand from a dust storm got into the gas tank. I'll get it fixed when I can."

"I'm out there often," I said, assuming she meant Palm Springs.

"Great. Why don't you come see me next time you're here? I'm going to be off work for the next few weeks. We can shoot for that."

"Off work?"

"I've got some bum joints. Surgery's scheduled for next week. They'll replace the knuckles on my right hand with plastic implants."

"I'm open weekend after next. I can drive out for a visit, and help you after the surgery. Two birds."

"That'd be swell."

"Why don't you email me the directions?"

"I'll just tell them to you now."

The thing is she didn't live in Palm Springs. When she said, "By Death Valley, near the Nevada border," I wanted to yank the offer back—pull my words right out of the phone wires. The name alone, Death Valley, smacked of danger. I imagined scorpions and vultures and crusty-skinned men carrying long-barreled rifles, shooting at empty beer cans and rattlesnakes. It was much further than Palm Springs and the opposite direction, to boot.

As each day passed, the regret telling her I'd come see her grew. An intuition□ a foreboding assisted by my normal, stressed, neurotic self□ convinced me we had nothing in common. That we never had.

Twice I picked up the phone to call with an excuse but didn't, because her call awakened something in me that'd been sleeping since my divorce□ a lightness.

My behavior was horrible during the split-up, and I felt out of touch with the world. Our friends sided with John. I thought a good deed might get my life back on track. Maybe I needed my old friend back. Or my childhood.

The thought of returning home was constant, but I drove on, as if powered by the menacing heat. Part of me was anxious to reminisce. To laugh lighthearted, like when we were little girls who wanted to ride on lightning bolts and shake hands with astronauts. Another part of me felt trapped in a web of politeness and the inability to say no.

Wind gusts shook the car. The wing of a moth flapped next to a yellow glob on the windshield. It reminded me of the insects Yvonne caught in elementary school from the windowsills above the stalls of the girls' bathroom. She'd rip one wing off and watch the creature thrash about the tiled floor, in circles.

Soon, bug debris was all over my brand new Jaguar. The heat and bleakness expanded with my anxiety. I reached for my cell phone to call Yvonne and beg off with an excuse. The signal was low, on its last bar. I scrolled through the menu for her number just as the truck Yvonne described came to view.

"You'll pass an old, rusty panel truck," she'd said. "Sittin' on concrete blocks. It's hard to miss. The word OOPS is spray painted across the side."

The word was huge and sloppy, with drips streaking down to the running board. A knot settled in my stomach as I passed by.

"Keep driving," she said. "Seventeen miles past the truck, turn right and keep going straight until you see the Shady Cabana Trailer Estates." I stuck the phone back in its holster and scolded myself for the panic attack.

When she told me she lived in a trailer park, I imagined one like my grandparents old vacation home. A two bedroom, doublewide, on a lush cliff overlooking the ocean, with comfortable patio furniture under an aluminum awning.

If it weren't for the prickly-pear garden and two plastic flamingos perched next to the hitch, Yvonne's runty trailer could have been abandoned. The cocoon shaped Airstream was pocked with dents. It looked crippled, supported by cracked, airless tires. A homemade sign next to the filmy louvered windows read "The Silver Twinkie."

The door opened. A woman filled the entrance. She had on a sleeveless muumuu. The color matched the blue painted on her puffy eyelids. I wasn't sure if it was Yvonne until she stepped into the garden and waved. The features of the girl I once knew were covered with swollen skin.

I pulled onto the pebbled drive behind a faded red Honda and adjusted the rear-view mirror to check my face, in the hopes that it hid the dread inside my chest. If only I'd listened to my intuition.

Yvonne made her way to my car. The contrast in our size was extreme. I got out, and we embraced. My cheek pressed against her muumuu, which smelled of sweat and mildew. I wished I'd worn something less tailored.

"Holy shit, Rosy, you look like a kid," she said and stepped back. "I'll be damned. You haven't changed one bit."

"Yvonne, it's nice of you to say that. And look at you. Where did you get that dress? Periwinkle's one of my favorite colors. It complements your eyes."

"Periwinkle? Hell, I just thought it was blue. Hey, that's one damn pretty set of wheels you're driving. What is it?"

I nodded and forced a smile, wishing, for the first time, I didn't have such a nice car.

"Come on inside," she said and offered her hand. A straight, healthy hand, fingers tipped with bright coral polish□ no bandages, or signs of surgery.

"Welcome to my abode." Yvonne opened the door. It gave a husky wine. "This here's a 1962 Globetrotter. They're hard to find anymore," she said, with a tone of pride. "I bought it from a couple of tin-can tourists who traveled just for fun. But Twinkie hasn't gone anywhere since I've owned her."

The linoleum floor bounced as if attached to springs, when we stepped inside. She closed the door tight. The swamp cooler droned. It seemed as if I could span the trailer from kitchen to sleeping area in five or six steps.

"Sit, sit, sit," she said, like she was training a puppy. I obeyed and sat on the tweed sofa behind a maple coffee table with an empty shoestring potato can on it. The heavy smell of pork and beans filled the space.

Yvonne sat across from me on an upholstered bench next to a worn Formica table.

"How long have you lived here?"

"Twenty years," she said. "This kind of living's not for everyone, but after a while it feels as comfortable as a mother's womb." Her words mixed with a laugh of short air blasts. "It's about the same size."

She reached in her pocket and pulled out a pack of cigarettes then stretched to grab an ashtray from the bookshelf next to her. An ice pick balanced on the top shelf. The words "Death Valley Ice Company" were stamped on the wooden handle in red block letters.

Instead of lighting up, she said, "My liver's startin' to rumble. You want to join us?"

"Us?"

"Usually it's just me and Jack." She got up and looked toward the kitchen area. A bottle of Jack Daniel's was on the counter by the sink. I checked my watch. It was close to two in the afternoon, and I hadn't been there five minutes. I don't drink before five.

"Sure," I said.

"Good."

The floor gave as she walked to the kitchen nook. The small, veneer cabinets above the sink were latched with oversized bobby pins fastened through eyehooks. Yvonne's muumuu filled the space. She poured us some Jack. No ice.

"Rosy, you see how easy things are when you live unpretentious?" Again, she laughed, noisy air mixing with her words.

Her manicured hands wrapped around the glasses. She set my drink on the maple table and plopped back on her bench. The Silver Twinkie closed in like a cage.

"I thought you were having surgery." I said.

"What surgery are you talking about?" One of her eyes twitched a little. "Damn, it's good to see you, Rosy. Let's drink to Peachgrove Street and to the 'friends-forever' bracelets we made." Yvonne shoved her meaty, formless wrist toward me. "Remember how we made these from the catgut in a tennis racket?" Her hand stayed put. "Remember how we'd share a roll of Lifesavers every Saturday, and promised-on-spit that nothing would come between us?

"Not really," I said. My head began to throb. I brought my hand to my forehead.

Her eye twitched again.

"Well that's real damn convenient, isn't it Rosy. I don't suppose you remember Skippy Howard either." Her voice slipped into a singsong juvenile tone.

"Skippy Howard?"

"You stole him from me with your brand new la-de-da bike. Your fancy Christmas present, with the streamers on the handlebars."

I laughed. "Yvonne?"

"Not funny, Rosy," she snapped. "How about Roger Jennings and Stevie Hinkle and Bobby Farley? I don't suppose you remember them either? You, strutting around in your peter-pan collars and angora socks, going off to cotillion with all the rich boys, while I stayed home."

"What's going on, Yvonne? Those were horrible boys. You were lucky you didn't have cotillion." I looked toward the door. "I always envied you getting out of those affairs. I wanted to be you and not have to go to them."

"Yep, you're still Miss Twist-Things-Around."

The sickly sweet smell of brown sugar bubbling in the pork and beans crawled up my nostrils. I thought, Jesus, how can I get out of here politely? I looked at the floor, to see brown spots on the linoleum. Perfectly round drips, like dried blood. Or it could have been sauce from the pork and beans.

"So, do you live here alone?" I said.

"Only since Larry died."

Our eyes met. My insides tightened. "Larry? Your husband?"

"Yep. Well, common law."

"That's okay."

"Larry was a loser. A real whack job." She took a sailor's gulp of Jack. "When we met, he drove a taxi. By the time we moved in together, he was a part-time drunk, a part-time bricklayer, and a full-time man of God."

"A man of God?"

"He was crazed with the Holy Scriptures." She shook her head. "His own damn version. He wasn't Baptist or Presbyterian or anything like that. He was a self-serving man of God with a Dodge Ram pulpit."

She put her hands in the air. Her voice dropped. "Praise be, God in heaven," she said. "Help my wife accept her journey of penance. Hold her hand as she walks through this life of purgatory. Lord Jesus, make her understand." Her speech pattern changed, as though she was channeling Larry and mocking him at the same time. "Let her know you intend her no harm, even though she is reminded everyday because she lives with the Devil's stupidity."

Yvonne leaned forward and coughed. White spittle collected in the corners of her mouth. I noticed movement past her shoulder, on the bookshelf. A roach crawled over the ice pick.

"He was an unpredictable freak, Rosy. I never knew what to expect next." She took another drink. "Every week brought seven days of damnation for the unclean spirits that dwell in us all. Myself in particular."

"Wow." I didn't know what else to say.

"He was a goddamn madman, Rosy."

Yvonne watched me reach for my purse and set it on my lap. My keys had been on top, but slipped inside with the sudden movement.

"What happened to him?" I tried to ask casually, but the words came out shaky.

"I was on the front porch watching him preach to no one from his truck bed. The Dodge rocked from his gyrations, like it'd been caught in its own little earthquake. He squealed about brimstone and the fire that never shall be quenched."

Yvonne's face began to pinch. I wanted to scream at the top of my lungs and bolt out the door right then, but was afraid it was locked.

My hand searched deep in my purse. The keys were nowhere.

"His face was gray as ash, and his arms were stretched out, fingers shaking like a son-of-a-bitch." She stood up to show me, and the Silver Twinkie moved.

"He was shouting to the Holy Ghost, and the veins in his neck jumped like they were trying to escape. One big fat vein finally burst. And Larry fell flat, choking on his own sermon."

I froze because of the way she stared at me.

"What did you do?" I asked fast.

"I made a joyful noise unto the Lord, Rosy. He'd finally given me a sign."

"Praise the Lord, Yvonne." I don't know why I said that. Then I added, "I guess God's looking out for you."

"You betcha, Rosy. And every day I thank him for taking Larry away."

The next thing Yvonne said was, "Now he's sent you back to me." She brought her hands together and rubbed them in a menacing gesture.

"Let's celebrate. More Jack?"

Without my answer, Yvonne took the ice pick from the book shelf and went to the kitchen. But Yvonne hadn't put ice in our last drinks.

"No more for me, thank you." I looked down at the brown dots on the floor again, convinced they were blood.

"Everything's just fine now," she said gently. "Now that I have you here."

I got up and ran to the door. It didn't budge. Yvonne turned.

"What are you doing, Rosy?"

Our eyes met. Her pupils looked microscopic inside the blue, puffed lids. She reached for my arm with a clammy hand. I breathed in her stench.

"You don't need to go anywhere, Rosy. Sit back down and visit awhile."

I stayed where I was. "For God's sake, Yvonne. You said you were having surgery. I came here to help you. I'm just here to help."

"I don't need no surgery." She smiled. "I said that to get you to come out. Don't you know, Rosy, I wanted to see you so bad. I didn't think you'd come unless I fibbed just a little. Hell, you're the one who taught me how to do that☐ fib just a little."

I jerked my arm from her soggy clutch. Yvonne stepped back. I thought I caught a glimpse of the ice pick in her far hand☐ the hand with the bracelet.

The surge of fear hit me as hard as if the ice pick had struck my temple. I screamed at the big blue monster that smelled bad—and punched my right fist deep into her belly, her enormous, gummy stomach. My hand hit a pillow of fat, and then the hard sack of intestines met my knuckles.

Yvonne fell back. Her head smacked on the corner of the bookshelf. Her menacing eyes turned empty. She slid to the floor. I moved the excess material of her muumuu with my shoe to look for the pick but only saw the dried blood drips and nothing else. The low-pitched growl of the swamp cooler turned haunting.

Yvonne tried to get up and then fell back, as if in a sound sleep. When I charged toward the door I saw the pick, the Death Valley Ice Company pick, still on the counter next to our glasses.

The door wasn't locked, just stuck. After two tries it scraped against the threshold when I shoved it open.

Once free from the Twinkie, I ran. The bite of a barrel cactus ripped through the leg of my pants. While stumbling toward the car I dug into my purse for the keys. They rattled, a maddening sound, but I couldn't feel them. My hand dug deeper tissues, half used matchbooks, a used toothpick. I set the bag on the hood of my car, looked back toward the Twinkie to make sure Yvonne was still inside, and frantically turned the bag upside down to empty the contents.

My wallet tumbled out. Credit cards and loose change slid under the car. Then everything else in the purse cascaded to the ground. The beautiful, life saving, Jaguar emblem on my keychain peeked out from a tear in the lining.

A throaty moan seeped from the Twinkie. The trailer swayed. Yvonne stumbled outside to the top step.

"Rosy," she called. "What are you doing? Please don't go. Please don't be mad at me."

"Get away from me," I screamed, as I got into my car. "Get away you sick, deceitful cow."

"Please don't go Rosy, please don't be mad at me!"

The key turned but stopped with the flat click of a faulty starter. It clicked and clicked, then nothing. Yvonne came down the steps. I locked the car and turned the key again. She reached for my door handle.

One last panic-filled try, and the engine whirled in a triumphant whine. I put the car in reverse. My foot shoved the pedal to the floorboard and the Jag roared backward.

Gravel battered the underside of the car as I sped to the highway, the moth wing still stuck, flapping on the windshield. The wind had died, and the world seemed to slow down. I rolled down the windows. The desert air dried my moist eyes as I accelerated past the panel truck on cement blocks with the word spray painted on the side. OOPS.

Please, Spring Morning

Marianne S. Johnson

Beyond the span of our morning campfire
in Anza-Borrego, the ocotillo lay prone as a dead king,
one root-leg in the earthen plane, the other, dry and
shrunken, still stretching toward mouth-watering sky.
I briefly stare at the grubby branches and the grip
of its thorns brazenly sprouting the first
early greens of the great mystery.
Look away, something says to me, look away.
Let spring come, let it come without trumpets.

Why I Married Him

Oriana Ivy

The only place in Milwaukee I loved
was a metal bridge downtown
that buzzed a low hum
under the wheels of cars.
I lived without music then, cut off

from nocturnes and the Rain Prelude,
but the bridge! It buzzed—
no, not like a giant bumblebee,
but only as a metal bridge can sing,
from the maws of Bethlehem Steel.

And he who was wrong for me—
anyone could see that—
he saw how I listened, and would make
a left turn, then a right,
and more astonishing left-rights.

It seemed to me that American men
had a compass in their heads,
and there we were, going over
the bridge again, me leaning down
to hear that burnished B flat,

that Opus Posthumous sound;
and to surprise me with delight,
he'd do it again, and off we went
over the metal bridge for the third,
fourth, fifth time. Who needed

roses when I had that hum
from the ores and depths. He saw
an orphan, and was feeding me
the only music there was,
that one nourishing note.

In a city where I could not speak
the language of the mind,
there was a humming bridge I loved;
and what can you do when you love
a bridge, except marry the driver.

Kingdom

Chau Matser

*T*he kingdom of America is lined with tall trees standing guard over smooth roads. How proud this country must be to lay strips of road from one city to the next, allowing even immigrants like Father and me deep into its forests. Father drives our used Chevrolet from our apartment to the wide blue lakes in the north. My two sisters and I in the back seat, I lift up my little wind-up camera and snap a picture through the top of the open window. A blurry print on film but I don't care. Through the camera, I see my world. Back in the city, our narrow building has a corner store where Father bought this camera. "My first gift in America," he says, "so you can report." He means "remember." My other sisters don't get anything, because I am his last wish for a boy that came as a girl. Even my name means both boy and girl. Inside me, there's a hope that my sisters don't have. When Father and Mother are old, my older sisters will be taking care of them. Me, I will be taking care of our dreams.

The trees slowly make room for a little town with little shops and screen doors. Father stops and buys a foam cup full of worms in fresh dirt. They wiggle and the dirt smells sweet. Father smiles at me, as I smell the dirt. I think that not being afraid of dirt is one of his dreams.

Cars line up alongside a grassy slope leading to the rocks. Jagged rocks, irregular and wide, that hang over the lake like a pier. It seems that Father is lucky today. He lifts up his long rod, one fish after another lying flat like paper. He wields his rod like a king's sword in command of the life in the lake. People place themselves on these rock piers, owning their rock, their rod, toolbox and bucket for their lucky catches. Father's fish lie on his rock, flapping their tails briefly before they lie quiet. My sisters and I run to the grass and trees, wrapping our legs around the scratchy bark trying to climb them, but their trunks are so wide, I can't. I run back to my camera lying in the grass.

He doesn't see the man approaching. The man is large, he's black, he's American. I know what Father thinks of blacks. No better than dirt, he's told us girls.

"Excuse me sir, how you doin' today?" says the man.

"What?" Father says. "What do you want?" Father whips his rod back to his chest, his elbow out.

"Well I'm fishin' over there, and my son and I walked into town. Have you seen a bucket on the rocks over there?" He points to the rock he had claimed with his son. To the rocks Father had climbed just minutes before. Where the man's bucket of fish was stolen and is now sitting next to Father.

"No," says Father. "I see nothing," There's almost a spit to the ground. A sound he makes in disgust.

The man's eyebrows are raised. "Well sir, that looks like my bucket you have there." His voice is unexpected. It is kind.

"No," Father says. This time he stops his hand and looks hard into the man's eyes. "I see nothing."

"You sure 'bout that?" The large man leans in, putting his hands on his hips. His head is shaking in rhythm to his words. He waits for a response. Father turns his whole body now to face him; the rod is swung down and stops between the man and the bucket. The space divided. The man lifts his right hand and points his thick finger to Father's chest, then stops. His hand falls back down. His head moves as if he is saying something more, but there are no sounds. There's just silence before he turns and walks back towards his son.

In the distance, I hear the son speak, "Does he have it?" he asks.

The large man nods yes.

The boy looks confused, but obediently follows his father back to their rock. I see them, but they don't see me. I've been watching them through my camera. My sisters are searching in the trees and I've been sitting on the grass between the rocks, waiting. I look down at the dirt between my feet. Dark, just like that man. I push my fingers into the dirt and it's soft. I look back to Father: elbow raised, rod across his chest, swinging it around his head. In one whip, he throws his line. Content. A bucket of swirling fish in water beside him. I put the camera down because, through it, I've seen the truth.

Voyeur

Una Nichols Hynum

Rilke says show angels the ordinary
as they show us the divine. I take my angels
to an abandoned house. I want them to see
how a house dies when deprived of human breath.
I point out the straw broom leaning against
a swayback screen, bindweed crawling
up the stairs. I show them puckered paint,
dust encrusted cobwebs. Taste the loneliness,
smell the absence. This is ordinary.
How like the angels I am, a voyeur,
looking in the window of the life which
I mistook for living. I take them to a funeral
to view the weeping violated faces. I tell them
the casket should have been smaller.

Catamarans

Anthony Bonds

It was a hot Sunday morning when Ursula snapped awake and announced to the family that she'd had a dream about sailboats. She said God was telling her to go to the bay while there was still time. Sundays mornings were usually for church, but Ursula's fervor for religion was matched, if not surpassed, only by her superstitiousness—especially when it came to dreams. She prepared sandwiches and darted back and forth across the crowded house collecting multiple bottles of sunscreen, towels, books, water bottles, and of course a camera.

"Is Feo coming too, mama?" Esteban asked, bouncing with excitement in his wheelchair. His enthusiasm for outdoor activities, and boats in particular, was one of the many things Ursula admired about her son. She was more of a quiet, reserved person, but Estaban was helping her learn how to be more effusive. It was staggering, the things she had learned from him, even though he had barely reached double digits.

"Can we bring him?" Esteban flashed a smile as a bribe.

Ursula looked at the dog's bowl and frowned. "Isabelle! Come to the kitchen please."

Isabelle, her oldest, crept sleepy-eyed from her room, headphones attached to her ears. She filled a glass of water at the sink and exhaled a long breath. "What?"

"You forgot to feed Feo again," said Ursula.

Isabelle looked at the food bowl remorselessly. "Seriously?" she said, turning back into her room.

Ursula gritted her teeth and made fists, but kept herself from lashing out in front of Esteban.

"Mama? Can we bring him this time?" Esteban repeated.

She opened a can of dog food and it dropped in the dog's bowl. Feo, an overweight pug-Chihuahua mix, limped to the bowl and licked the brown lump of food with his dry tongue, his milky eyes wandering blindly. "Sorry, *mijo*. Not today. He's old and needs rest," she said.

Ursula was convinced that Feo and Esteban had a cosmic connection because they'd been born on exactly the same day. They had grown up together, discovered the world together, and once Feo was old enough, he became very protective of his human companion. Though it pained her to think about it, she had always felt that once one of them passed away, the other would not be far behind.

Esteban whistled. Feo usually responded by wagging his tail wildly and licking Esteban's toes, but now he was mostly deaf, with barely the stamina to stand firm while his slow tongue lapped the clumps of food.

"Isabelle!" Ursula shouted through the bedroom door once all the preparations had been packed into the car. "*Vamanos!*" For ten whole minutes Ursula argued through the door with Isabelle, who didn't want to go to the bay. She said flatly that she had other plans. Ursula spoke sharply as a snake, enumerating her daughter's most recent shortcomings. "And if you agree to feed the dog, feed the dog!" she shouted. "You know how much that dog means to him. If Feo goes, you know what will happen? Esteban will die of a broken heart, that's what will happen. And it will be on your head, *niña!*" Even at the time, Ursula knew it was a horrible thing to say to her daughter, but that didn't make it less true.

Huffing, Ursula ushered Esteban out to the car, buckled him in, collapsed his chair into the trunk, and said, "Your sister's not coming." Then she hollered to the house, "She's an important *mujer* all of a sudden, too busy with all her boyfriends to even say goodbye!" Isabelle, still inside, gave no audible response. Curtains shifted in neighboring windows and Ursula lurched the car away.

At the bay, they found a shady spot with a picnic table and Ursula flipped the brake levers on Esteban's chair. She regretted forcing him to wear a cheap sombrero that made him look like a mariachi cartoon, but the doctor said that every precaution must be taken to protect his skin from the sun.

Sitting on the bench, she broke off pieces of a peanut butter and jelly sandwich and fed them to Esteban. He still had some motor movement in his hands, but he couldn't do sandwiches anymore. He chewed slowly and needed frequent sips of water to help him swallow.

The crystal blue water in the bay was streaked with the wakes of yachts, motorboats, and, thanks be to God, catamarans.

"Mama, look, catamarans!"

"Lots of them today," she said.

"You know why catamarans have two hulls? It's so they can go faster than regular sailboats. And they can do better tricks."

"Be sure to chew." Ursula made him drink from the water bottle.

"For real. Papa told me."

"I know, *mijo*."

Sailing was the only thing he ever talked to Esteban about. The man had always wanted to buy a catamaran, but they never had the money—first there was the recession, then his boss cut his hours, then Esteban got sick. He must have thought he deserved a medal for sticking around as long as he did, a whole year after the diagnosis. Then one day, like a fickle wind, he and all of his possessions vanished from the house. Not long after that Ursula was served with divorce papers. She never asked for an explanation.

Ursula and Esteban watched the boats for hours until the heat of the day had soaked her blouse through. She was tossing sandwich wrappers and empty water bottles into a canvas bag when her cell phone chimed.

It was Isabelle. She was crying.

Esteban's sombrero had fallen into his lap. Even though the sun was setting and the protection was no longer necessary, he pawed it with his hands, trying to pick it up.

Ursula stepped away, out of earshot. "What's wrong?"

"Mama?" said Isabelle. Her usual listlessness had been replaced by genuine fear. "It's Feo. Something's not right. He's not getting up."

"Maybe he's just asleep," she said.

"No, Mama, I think he's…"

Ursula sighed and touched her forehead. It was warm from sun exposure.

"What should I do?" the girl asked.

"We're coming home right now," said Ursula.

"I'm sorry, Mama."

"*Mija*, listen to me very carefully. It's not your fault."

Ursula returned to her son and smiled, praying that it would appear convincing. She knew this could well be their last trip to the bay. In recent weeks Esteban's condition had worsened—he had not slept, his hair was falling out in whole patches now, and he could barely keep even the blandest food down.

"Who was it Mama?"

Ursula turned her head so he wouldn't see that her eyes had welled up. The low sun streaked the water, rippled by crisscrossing wakes of catamarans not yet ready to call it a day.

Blinking away the sting in her eyes, she replaced the floppy hat onto Esteban's head, her hand lingering on his thin neck as she sat down on the bench.

"Let's watch the boats, *mijo*," she said, "just a little longer."

What I Know

Judith Barkley

Beneath a fierce sun
Wilson's and Red-necked Phalaropes,
the size of a man's hand,
snatch brine flies in mid-air
and from the lake's surface.
They're on their way to South America.
"We might well be envious of them," you say,
as we walk single file, you in front,
along the shore of Mono Lake.
Yet we both know that each soft step
we take in this tender landscape
says we wish to be nowhere else.
You are wearing your favorite leather hat;
I note how it is faded
and, like your hair, gray now.
We know some day our journeys here
will end. We will huddle,
pull our sweaters tighter
as winter approaches
sooner every year. But today,
it is still summer,
the sun still fierce.

Hard Work and a Clean Spirit

Nicole Vollrath

*A*ppalachians named our town Desperation for a reason. Bad guys descend on it the hour they get paroled, thumbing rides from migrant workers, then demanding their wallets at knifepoint. Criminal elements have brawls at Jacob's Ladder, the straight bar in town, and have messed up so many patrons of the Glass Slipper, Floyd Willis boarded it up and fled to Miami "to retire."

Desperation's down-and-out men meet hard-luck women and spawn kids no better off. Every smart, young, fresh-from-college teacher bribed to come here gets a rude education in we-got-no-use-for-queer-ideas and you-may-think-you're-better-'n-us-but-this-bat-smacking-your-Volvo-says-otherwise. Fancy degrees aren't required to cripple your back at the Winston mine, intimidate clerks at the welfare office, or trade food stamps for paper-bag whiskey.

Guys like me, lousy at sports with a preacher for a dad, don't count for much. "Hard work and a clean spirit is all you need to make a good life," Pop says. I don't see it, though. Jessie Winkler's the sweetest girl I know, but she still got raped by the Dillard gang leaving a party she never should have gone to. Kid was left for dead in a snow bank three miles off road. "Lucky to be alive," the cops and my father kept saying, as if the stunning part of the story is her survival, not the brutality that put her there.

Me, I lay low as a shadow, with perfect attendance. No one in our aging congregation doubts I'll earn my high school diploma—myself included—but four years feels like a life sentence. Our nightly prayers before supper and bed are just words to me. "Please God, get me out of here," is what repeats in my mind after every fresh tragedy in the Coal County Tribune. Quentin Nash: Desperation High's star quarterback, paralyzed by a drunk driver. Ryan Rhodes: overdosed on heroin Easter weekend. Samantha Patterson: gave birth in the locker room during spirit week, and girls say you can still see stains on the concrete floor. Tell myself "Jesus loves me" and "One more year" and "I will survive," crossing both sets of fingers until my knuckles bruise. Unless you've served time in this town, you don't know that fear can shrink you so small, you can't find yourself in the mirror.

"Violence never solved a thing," Pop tells the mug shot of the man who stabbed a church deacon for stepping on his lawn. Wants me to know how proud he is of me, his good son, for turning the other cheek and resisting youthful vices so many, many times. X, cocaine, and crystal meth were found on half the kids at senior prom, I read the morning after.

You probably guessed that I did not attend. Zooming off to Florida in a rented tuxedo and borrowed car seemed a better way to celebrate four years of prayers come true.

the composer

Jackson Crow-Mickle

he slowly twisted
the strings into rope,
a collection of As, Ds, and Cs
rendered into a single moment
before sunset,
where his concerto captured
the green note
from the knife edge of the horizon.

he recreated the moment
when we knew
we knew nothing,
when our maps
were filled with vibrant myths
that the blank edges
could hardly contain.
when rocks and whirlpools
still possessed a spark of the imagination,
before Edison caged them all
in crystal balls,
to enlighten us
through every unwaking moment
our eyes are open.

and knowing all that
we had lost all of that,
he toiled at his bench
fashioning the pinprick of sound
that in the instant
when we blink our eyes
all world could remember
the glories still existing
in the remnants of music.

Stone Cricket

Susan Union

*T*he cavalier way Michael banged the metal legs of his folding chair together when he set it down made Claire bite her lip until she tasted blood. He acted as if they were at a damn Little League game or attending a sunset concert in the park.

Beyond a chain-link fence, the highway flowed with a whine of engines as a steady stream of commuters headed home to their families and to their children.

"Need help?" Michael asked.

"No." She put her chair close to his, but not touching, and forced herself to sit. A strand of hair clung to her lips before it broke free. Lipstick seemed absurd under the circumstances, but it held what was left of her together. She clenched her teeth to keep them from chattering as the air whipped the tops of the pines. Should have brought a sweater, Claire thought. The sun won't be out much longer.

She gave a nod to the elderly couple sitting five feet to her left and lifted her chin to the rest of the gathering scattered around the expanse of freshly mowed grass.

"Listen." The old man leaned forward and wiggled the brim of his faded cap. "Crickets."

Claire shook her head. He was wrong. Crickets meant that all was right in the world, that everything was as it should be. There were no crickets here. The only insects in this place were the ants that scurried through her veins.

"Jiminy," he said with a voice that contradicted a face creased with wear.

The woman at his side spread a blanket over her legs and rubbed vigorously. Claire wondered if the woman's body teemed with ants too, or if she'd already passed that stage.

"'Bout three weeks you've been coming here?" The man addressed his question to Michael. "The wife and I didn't want to bother you, but some of the others asked."

"Breezy this evening," Michael replied. "Smells like rain."

"It gets easier after a while." The man removed his cap and smoothed what remained of his hair. "All in all, we're a good group of folks."

"Lord knows we understand each other," his wife said. "Not many do. At Christmas, we exchange gifts and we'll have a potluck or two in the summer."

A gust stirred the nearby branches, and a flash of yellow caught Claire's eye. She held her breath, but the movement of color belonged only to Pooh Bear swinging like an ornament from a nearby tree. Each time Pooh banged the bark, Claire winced inside.

"We've been wondering..." The man clasped his wife's hands, covering them completely with knobby knuckles. "What happened?"

Michael opened his mouth to reply, then reclined, legs stretched and crossed at the ankles, beer in hand. It wasn't his fault, of course, but Claire wanted to pound him with her fists.

The man shifted on his seat. There was a soft popping noise as the chair leg broke through the turf. He turned so that his knees touched those of his wife and gave a nod to the blue heart-shaped stone beyond his ancient work boots. "Our boy..." The man's voice caught and his wife picked up, ". . . was five."

"You keep coming here," the man said, "you'll feel better—someday."

Claire forced herself to look at the stone in front of her and Michael as the last flash of sunlight glinted off the pink marble. She rose from her chair, but before she could stand, she felt her knees give out. Michael's arm was there before she hit the ground, wrapped around her waist, holding her up. She caught his eye, challenging him to falter, to crack. She held his gaze until the wind dried her eyes to bone, and he held hers.

Michael stroked her shoulder, heat seeping from his fingers. "I miss," he whispered, "the smell of her hair."

The distant roar of rush hour traffic dwindled to a trickle. Michael held her until the neighboring couple and the rest of the others were long gone. "Ready?" he asked at last, easing his arm from her back.

Claire took a deep breath as they gathered their things. The ants had slowed to a crawl, and when Michael collected his chair from the grass, instead of the clang of metal bars, Claire heard the far away chirping of crickets.

jazz is e.e. cummings

Debbie Hall

jazz is a flash of sheet lightening
zigzagging
down a granite face

when it hits the river
it swims upstream
and startles a herd of cattle
lapping at water's edge

they low
a Billy Holiday lament
and start swaying

as the hawk overhead
lets loose in a soprano sax
and the deer scatter
in syncopated notes

of panic, *but it's just jazz*
croons the wind,
and don't you know, jazz
is e.e. cummings

he's a friend
and the wind turned things
over to the sun (don't worry)
who soothed the fearful

(not wholly) convinced
but then came the fog and the mist
who caressed them
with Moody's Mood for Love

yes yes (feel it now)
jazz is moon kissing swallows
in minor keys splashing
out of Coltrane's heart

onto the rocks where the sirens
call cometomamanow
(*may I feel?* said he)

Son of Hell

Scott Barbour

When the new kid stepped into The Arena of Pain, we all fell silent. The new kid wasn't like us.

What was like us?

Like us was King Murder, a six-foot-three, 257-pound, tenth-grade flunky with a Burger King crown on his shaved head.

Like us was El Muerte, a poor Hispanic kid with a pillowcase *lucha libre* mask.

Like us was me, Zarathustra, an over-tested underachiever sacking out at my grandma Phyllis's prefab.

The new kid lived in a two-story house on Piedmont. His mom drove a Jag, his dad a BMW. He was an honor student who did volunteer work. He had clear skin and manners.

We watched the new kid inspect the ring, a five-foot-by-seven-foot sheet of warped, blood-stained plywood in the middle of The Arena of Pain (that is, Phyllis's backyard). The ring had no ropes, just an aluminum ladder next to it for moves that required elevation.

The girls whispered and laughed at—what? His plaid shirt? His creased slacks? His probable virginity?

The new kid wandered among the props scattered in the yard—pots and pans, a table leg, a crowbar. He was trailed by the dog-boys, a pack of long-haired, semi-domesticated twelve-year-olds who'd shown up during a late-July heat wave and kept coming back. They were not allowed in the ring, but they were given important jobs, like managing the props and cueing up the ring-entrance theme songs on the boom box.

"Who are you?" the black-haired dog-boy asked.

The new kid approached the ladder and began to climb. The dog-boys rushed to hold the ladder steady, one at each of its four legs, just as they'd been trained. The new kid stood poised at the ladder's apex and lifted his arms to the sky. "I am Son of Hell!" he shouted. "My evil knows no bounds!"

Then he dove headfirst to the plywood.

Several weeks later, after his stitches and neck brace were removed, Son of Hell returned and asked for a match. I turned him down on grounds of mental instability, but the other members of the Fort Smith Wrestling Federation lobbied on his behalf.

"We're all fucking loco," said El Muerte. "That's the whole point."

King Murder cracked his knuckles and smirked. "Yeah, give the kid a shot."

In the ring, Son of Hell was never satisfied. When El Muerte hit him in the face with a cookie sheet and gave him a bloody nose, Son of Hell wanted a frying pan to the back of his head.

When the Bloody Fist leveled him with a flying clothesline and followed up with a diving stomp, Son of Hell demanded to be knocked semiconscious and dragged through broken glass and rusty nails.

After The Tornado of Grief poked him in the eye, kneed him in the groin, slammed him onto his back and elbow-dropped his chest, Son of Hell begged for a tilt-a-whirl backbreaker or a spinning crucifix toss, followed by a fist drop to the forehead.

It didn't take long to realize Son of Hell really wasn't like us; he was better, a true showman offering up his body for extreme abuse again and again.

I couldn't help wondering where his need for pain came from. I suspected the answer lay in his name. What form of hell spawned him in that house on Piedmont? I never asked, and he didn't talk much, except to ask for increasingly dangerous props and to teach us the moves he needed us to use on him.

Son of Hell kept demanding a championship match against King Murder, the undisputed champion of the FSWF. King Murder's thirst for inflicting pain was as extreme as Son of Hell's need to receive it. The idea of putting them in the ring together terrified me, but the public demanded entertainment, high drama.

The match was held on a rainy late-November Thursday. Son of Hell entered the ring in his trademark creased slacks, plaid shirt, and deck shoes. No music. No theatrics. Just a skinny kid with wavy hair and dark eyes standing in the rain. The red-haired dog-boy cued up England's national anthem on the boom box, and King Murder strode regally into the Arena of Pain through Phyllis's backdoor. He wore short pants and no shirt, his Burger King crown on his head, and a child's Halloween-costume king's robe across his shoulders.

As soon as the bell rang, King Murder picked Son of Hell up over his head, slammed him to the mat, and fell on him with a cross body slam. Next, he swung Son of Hell around by his ankles five times, releasing him into the ladder.

All the moves I'd worked out, along with the dialogue and dramatic interludes, were nowhere to be seen.

Son of Hell served himself up to be punched, kicked and thrown, over and over. He called out for props—not for him to use, but for King Murder to use on him. "Chair! Baseball bat! Chain! Ice pick!"

Fortunately, even the dog-boys refused that request, scratching their heads as they pretended not to know what an ice pick was.

In the third and final round, just as I thought he might survive, his body bruised and bleeding but his limbs still functioning, Son of Hell shouted, "Bowling ball!"

The blond-haired dog-boy unzipped the oddly shaped bag, lifted out my grandpa's red Brunswick, and lugged it into the ring. King Murder took the ball, raised it above his head with both hands, and straddled Son of Hell's prone body.

"How dare you challenge King Murder!" He shouted. "King Murder is the champion of all time!" He stood with the ball held high above Son of Hell's head.

Son of Hell lay on his back with his eyes closed, his hands across his chest, his face a mask of pure tranquility, as King Murder stood poised with the ball, sixteen pounds of blunt force, wet and glistening and crimson under the gray winter sky.

Inhaling Poetry

Regina Morin

After all,
it's the scent of a poem
that lingers:
the pungent musk of Bukowski,
the hint of tobacco from Whitman,
Anne Sexton's peppered ambergris,
bitter and beguiling.
Can you smell a hint
of splashed coffee wafting from
that Billy Collins poem, or is it
a nice Chianti as he bites
the face off yet another
metaphor?
I've opened a summer melon
only to let the sweetness of Neruda
arise from its green hollow and
as the dark cinnamon
sifts into a silky batter,
Dickinson's somber face
appears.

A Few Small Repairs

Richard Farrell

Jimbo leans out from beneath the propped-open hood and presents a piece of engine to you, a cold, gray metal thing with no real form. He tries to include you, holding up the parts of his car one after another, as if you have some hidden expertise. But they all look the same to you, just dull iron shapes, which of course they are, whatever they are, until they're doing their thing inside the engine. Dissected and removed, everything loses significance. You wonder about what they're going to do with the pieces of you after surgery.

In the garage with Jimbo, you find ways to appreciate his enthusiasm about the Chevette—carburetors, spark plugs and compression ratios—but with a layman's courtesy, with the same smile, the same bland-but-polite interest you gave your oncologist on that first visit when he told you he'd trained at a Midwestern hospital that you'd never heard of but that your ex-sister-in-law nurse, Deb, had. And it was a "damn-fuck good one" according to Deb, top three for cancer surgery, which comforted you some when you saw Dr. Rasley next in the La Jolla office, surrounded by his framed diplomas, and listened to him explain how he would excavate your pelvis. It's like that with Jimbo and this car, the boyish pleasure he takes while trying again to attach something called a "Holley 2-barrel carburetor" onto the metallic orange, 1979 Chevette he's been restoring for six months. He promises to drive you in it, across the country and back to your old house in Vermont, once the seats are back from the upholstery shop and the chemo's finished and you're "better," whatever that means—no uterus and no ovaries—but better. He wants to leave the kids with his parents, to drink beer with you, to swim in a lake and fish with you. He wants to drive you around town and visit your old high school and make love in the backseat along the highways of America. But Jimbo can't make that carburetor fit, even though he's checked the part number four times and he's called the parts dealer and he's taken it off and put it on and taken it off again. He's excited about it though, the challenge of it. The failures don't bother him. And you're comforted by this too, his quest to restore an old car to its pristine state. His dedication, like your doctor's pride about diplomas, reassures you that the world continues while your body cannibalizes itself. These things matter. You know that. You really are happy for your husband, because tinkering on an old car makes him so happy.

Though you'd be happier if he'd offer to cook dinner for the kids, clean the dishes or just give you a break for an hour or two and let you get your nails done, or meet Deb for a fish taco and a margarita at the little place down in Ocean Beach. He doesn't understand that you need a few hours each day to deal with everything you're dealing with, and there's so much to do before the surgery and before the chemo even starts.

"Look at that," Jimbo says pulling out a glob of grease from the engine. "How did I not see this? It must've been blocking the threads."

And you think the same thing, how the hell did you not see the future when you horse traded your freedom and hitched your wagon to Jimbo? But now you're being morose. He's a good father and you still love him, which after eighteen years is a damn spot better than a lot of your friends can say. But then you remember Dr. Rasley and the diplomas, you keenly anticipate the operation and the chemo and the buckets of vomit, and you suddenly want to smash your foot into the Chevette's orange quarter panel and destroy Jimbo's happiness. And you start to move toward doing it, too, anticipating the thrill, your toes crumpling the smooth edges, the afterglow of a dent marring that glossy, pumpkin finish, all that time Jimbo spent in the garage while your cells devoured one another. Jimbo must see it in your eyes, too, because he stands up, rushes to you.

"What wrong?" he says.

"What's wrong?" you say. "What's wrong?"

He nods his head.

"The color sucks," you say. "It looks like puke. Who the hell paints a car orange?"

He sulks. You feel like screaming, like running away down to the ocean or up into the mountains, but you know you won't. You'll stand here and take it. You'll take whatever's coming.

"It's going to be okay," Jimbo says. He holds out his grease-stained palms but you slap them away. He steps closer and pulls you in.

"I want them," you say.

"You want what? What do you mean?"

"I want them," you say again. "I want to keep my ovaries."

A week later, you awake numb in a sterile room. You expect pain, agony really, but everything is numb. Machines ping and beep around you, but even these noises seem distant and detached. Something went wrong, you think. Somehow the doctor severed your spine, though your feet work and your hands move, you just can't feel them.

You stay like this for a long time, hours perhaps. It's hard to say since time, too, has lost its thread. A second could be a year. There's no clock in this pale room. Then another thought: perhaps you're really dead. Since you aren't sure what death will feel like, this very well could be it. Eternity spent numb and frozen in a white room. What the hell did you expect?

After dark, sensations slowly return, but still no pain. And though this is an impossible contradiction—after all they've torn open your abdomen and ripped out your insides—the lack of pain continues.

You ask the nurse why there's no pain. You ask him why no one is visiting you and why the toes on your left foot feel like they're on fire. The nurse answers, but his words don't make sense. It's only when Jimbo enters that you think, perhaps, you've survived.

"It doesn't hurt," you say. "It's supposed to hurt, but it doesn't. Why is that?"

Jimbo shrugs his shoulders, bends down, kisses your cheek. His lips are warm.

Pain never arrives. There's only tightness down there, something akin to a good stomach workout, but no pain. It's eerie, like the incision carved out by the surgeon's scalpel is growing into a black hole and sucking the rest of your body down. You begin to crave pain. You worry that the lack of pain means something else is wrong, that perhaps they removed more than your reproductive apparatus; that perhaps they removed the core of you.

The reassuring Dr. Rasley comes in and reassures you.

"There's no pain," you say to him.

"Some patients respond better to meds than others," he says.

"They pay you for this?" you say. The doctor smiles and leaves the room. Jimbo watches him go with a stunned expression on his face.

On the day you're set to go home, Jimbo comes to retrieve you. He's holding a paper bag with loop handles. He looks nervous, unsure about what to do as he turns, peeks down the hall, closes the door, then walks around the far side of your bed and draws the thin curtain around. You begin to wonder if this is really your husband or some nervous approximation of him, a dream that you can't come out of.

"I have something for you," Jimbo says. Then he reaches into the paper bag and removes a glass jar.

It appears to be from a high school science lab, with a thick, black cap and metrical gradations on the glass. Inside, two tiny objects float like de-shelled oysters in a yellowy liquid.

"Tell me those aren't what I think they are," you say. The sight of your organs makes you momentarily queasy.

Jimbo smiles. "Take 'em," he says. He looks around again as if he's pulled off a crime. "I had to convince two hospital lawyers and a medical ethicist before they'd sign a release. They think I'm nuts."

"Why?" you say.

He shakes the jar and the tiny white globs slosh around inside. He smiles and hands it to you. For the first time since you've awoken from surgery, you feel a sensation in your palms as you grasp the jar.

"You said you wanted to keep them."

"Jesus," you say. "They're so small."

You wonder what to do with the jar and your ovaries. Part of you wants to throw them away, but you're afraid it's morbid just to dump them in the trash. Or you could keep them, next to the shoebox of Gilly's teeth beneath your bed. Of course, ovaries aren't teeth. Frankie had that mole removed last year from his back and you didn't ask for it, so maybe your ovaries are more like Frankie's mole and you should just throw them away. After Frankie arrived, Jimbo didn't want more kids and you agreed, more or less, so what will you do with two ovaries? Will you stare at them like those floating cat fetuses in Gilly's biology classroom? "Gross," she calls them.

Everything is gross to Gilly now: your graying hair is gross, your sagging boobs, your tuna casserole, your cancer. Gilly sees the world only in pristine states, and anything complicated, anything that requires effort away from mirrors or cell phones, is gross. Your ovaries would be gross, too, except maybe she'd be right on that one. Maybe gross would accurately describe the jar and its contents.

The summer burns, hot and dry. Wildfires in the mountains fill the air with heavy ash. Days, weeks go by. Your family tiptoes around the house like they are in church.

When Jimbo and the kids start back to school in late August, you begin the first round of chemo. You lose weight, slouch around the house in slippers and bathrobes. Hair falls out in clumps and clogs the shower drains. Deb attends to you during the day. In spite of the divorce, Deb still lives with Frogman, Jimbo's brother. They've remained, indescribably, a sort of couple. She holds your hair back while you retch, boils ginger in your tea and packs the kids' lunches. Frankie's tenth birthday comes and goes with only a twenty-minute quasi-celebration in the kitchen—four cupcakes and a single candle. Everyone accommodates your disease. You become a marksman in the bathroom, learning to center-mass the commode with your vomit and diarrhea, hardly splattering the sides anymore. Friends and neighbors keep sending food, as if you are a child trapped in a well, but most of it goes to waste. The kitchen brims with casseroles, vats of spaghetti, lasagna, pot roasts, plates of cookies, fruit trays, and loaves of bread. Christ, you could eat for a month with all the food your friends have sent. Gilly refuses everything except shrimp and peanut butter. Frankie becomes taciturn. Following his father's example, he keeps saving the leftovers for you, your ten-year-old already acquainting himself with the male panacea for suffering: silence and more food.

After a while, it seems normal to have your ovaries under the bed, next to the shoebox of Gilly's teeth. You pull the jar out when the house is empty and hum Shawn Colvin tunes. For some reason, the sight of the jar puts you in a singing mood. You begin to notice the beauty of your ovaries, the intricacies of their shape, the folds and ridges, the little frayed edges of tissue. You can see the sharp cuts where the surgeon snipped them free. The more you examine your organs, the more you think that you are gazing into a corner of your soul. They change color and dimension during the different times of day. In the morning, when sunlight slants into the room, they are nearly diaphanous. They glow in the first cusp of evening. In the witching hours, you detect the faintest echoes of songs coming from the jar, rising out of the fluid like a whispering chorus of ten thousand harmonized voices while the world and your family sleeps.

You want desperately to take them out of the preservative, but you're convinced that if you start doing this, you won't be able to stop. They'll spoil quickly in air. You give serious thought to swallowing them, to bringing them back inside your body, and are unsure what stops you.

You also recognize that you might be cracking up.

The heat is relentless. A steady Santa Ana blows through the fall. Records are set. You turn the air conditioner down to sixty-four, but can't get cool.

The car seats take longer than expected but finally arrive in October. Jimbo and Frankie carry them inside and then drag you out to the garage to see them. Jimbo is covered in sweat. Two front bucket seats and a larger bench for the back, the most expensive items in the restoration process, balance on metal frames. They look good. You're surprised by this, how the seats change your opinion of the car, and how the car changes your opinion of Jimbo, and how your opinion of Jimbo changes your opinion of yourself. You feel a twinge of something, a precancerous memory perhaps, or the first flicker of hope. The upholstery is creamy white with the Chevy bow-tie emblem stitched in the center.

"Try 'em out," Jimbo says to you. Frankie smiles with his dad's pride. "You'll be the first to sit in them."

"Why does it matter so much to you?" you say. "It's just an old car, a clunker really. A Chevette? Couldn't you have restored a Lincoln?"

"The simple things matter," Jimbo says. He's crouched next to the car, preparing it for the insertion of the seats. "You know that."

Jimbo wipes his forehead, smearing sweat and grease above his thick eyebrows. A real grease monkey, except that he's not. He teaches high school history and writes letters to the editor in his spare time. Gilly worries about being in his class next year. "Gross," she says, "my dad as my teacher." But you know she doesn't mean it. You know secretly she's hoping it works out. They're close, Gilly and her dad, closer than you've ever been with her. Both kids love Jimbo best.

Frankie sits down next to you in the other bucket seat and pats your knee. Your son doesn't understand about your hair-robbing illness. The seat creaks, wobbling on metal braces. In the sweltering garage, it's quiet. No one knows what to say to you. The only honest voices you hear come from inside that jar. And they say you're dying.

Until this moment, you've said nothing to Jimbo about the black hole in your pelvis and how it grows each day, allowing your husband to keep believing in the healing power of socket wrenches, chemotherapy, and time.

"I'm not getting better," you say. "It's eating me alive." Frankie lifts his hand off your knee. Then you add, "Frankie, do you want to see momma's jar?"

You're not sure where this comes from. Jimbo turns and glares at you.

"Go inside, Frankie" he says.

"Don't dismiss him," you say. Your son starts to get up but you hold him back.

"It was a mistake," Jimbo says. He's back sitting inside the seat-less car. "Throw them away."

"I won't," you say. You cling to Frankie. "It's empty inside me, like I'm falling into myself. They took too much, Jim. They took the essence of me. All I have left is in that jar."

You wonder how your family will remember these times when you're gone.

A week later, on the first cool morning in months, a thick marine layer blanketing the coast, you fish one of the ovaries out with a spoon and touch the tip of your tongue to it. It tastes rancid, like rotting milk mixed with gasoline, but touching it, tasting it is thrilling beyond anything you've ever experienced.

You drop the ovary back into the jar, call Deb and tell her not to come over. Then you grab the Chevette keys. You drive along the San Diego coastline as the gray clouds burn off, evaporating into patches of blue. Waves roll toward the shore then collapse in frothing foam. You haven't felt the ocean in over a year, so you park. Carry the jar down to the surf and dip your toes in. The salty water splashes against your legs and milky, gasoline flavors come back to you like dreams. Nearby, flies swarm around a rotting patch of brown kelp, but the ocean shimmers. You clutch the jar close and consider throwing it into the waves.

You drive east from the coast, the jar buckled in the creamy passenger seat, ascending toward distant, purple-brown mountains. The heat returns, climbing with each inland mile, and the sun beats down on the orange hood. Black scars from wildfires mottle the horizon. Your back sweats against the still-stiff car seat, but the engine revs smoothly, vibrating tiny concentric waves on the formaldehyde surface, lapping against sides of the jar. You drive up into the foothills that separate the city from the desert, racing the car along narrow, windy roads. You've never felt so free.

You park again, this time in a small mountain town. You order apple pie and bourbon for lunch. The air is cooler, autumnal and the bourbon settles your stomach. The jar is in your purse. After a second drink, you take the jar out and place it on the table. You no longer care what anyone thinks.

California transforms into Vermont. Golden leaves swirl in the breeze and the bourbon swirls with your Zofran. Crisp, fall sunlight stretches your shadow across the sidewalk and into the street as wood-smoke floats overhead. "I could die here," you think, but then you realize you've said this out loud, apparently to the jar. A plump waitress with pigtails and tattoos on her arms brings you another drink and looks warily at it.

"My ovaries," you say to her.

"Cool," she says. She pulls down her skirt's waistband, revealing white and puckered skin. She touches her finger along a blanched scar. "I have my appendix at home."

You wonder if you've just stumbled upon some weird legion of organ hoarders, imagining websites, T-shirts, and annual meetings.

Sometime after your fourth bourbon and third piece of apple pie, you call Jimbo. Two hours later, he takes you home in the SUV, Frogman trailing in the Chevette.

"No more," Jimbo says. The jar is in the back seat. "No more."

You make the rest of the return trip in awkward, drunken silence.

The last round of chemo drips into your veins on the first full day of winter. The black hole inside your body almost fills you up, from your knees to your neck. There's so little left. Jimbo collects you in front of the clinic. You're happy to see him until you slide inside his bright orange Chevette and he hands you a bottle of Champagne.

"You did it," he says.

"Don't talk to me," you say. "Take me home."

A few days later, Deb walks in and finds you asleep on the couch, the jar resting on your chest. She is holding it in her hands as you open your eyes.

"They're eerie," she says.

You stare at her a moment. You no longer recognize her. Acid rises in your throat.

"Get the fuck out of my house," you say. Your voice is calm, even, and unequivocal. You snag the jar from her trembling hands.

That night, brushing your teeth, you see Jimbo's reflection kneeling at the side of your bed, and before you can stop him, he slides out the jar.

"Get rid of these," he says, holding it up.

You throw a glass cup at his head but miss. It shatters. Shards crackle around his feet. You want him to scream, to fight back, to throw the ovary jar, but he doesn't. He just stands there in the silent aftermath until Gilly rushes in. She's wearing pink pajamas and an orthodontia wire wrapped around her face. Jimbo rotates the jar behind his back.

"It's fine, honey," he says in a soothing voice to Gilly. "Just a broken glass."

Gilly watches you with wild, angry eyes.

"What's going on?" she says.

"I'm disappearing," you say. "It's eating me alive. I can feel it."

"Stop that," he says. Gilly watches from the door. "The doctor said it's not spreading. You need to get rid of these things. They're making you nuts."

"I need them," you say. "I need them more than I need you."

Your daughter's face begins to quiver.

"I'm serious," Jimbo says, anger rising for the first time in months. "If you won't do it, I will."

"It will be the last thing you do," you say. For the second time that day, you snatch the jar from the hands of someone you love.

By Christmas, the doctors regulate your meds enough for you to apologize to Deb. She hugs you but is reluctant. Your friendship will never be the same. Jimbo takes the Chevette keys with him when he leaves. You can smell your children again—the orange flavor of Gilly's acne cream, Frankie's sweaty-ball-cap hair. You hadn't smelled them since summer. Jimbo's found an old Airstream camper that he wants to restore and Frankie desperately wants to help. "I'll put it in the alley," Jimbo says to you.

"Do whatever you want," you say, but you take no pleasure in hurting him. If you've learned nothing else, it is the limitlessness of Jimbo's compassion. He deserves better, but you can't find the "nice" button anymore, and you resent the hell out of his heroic and chaste servitude to your disease.

The emptiness inside begins to recede, though no part of you believes that you're getting better. If the blackness inside your hips wasn't Death, then it was Death's cousin.

On New Year's Eve morning, Jimbo drives out to Lakeside to inspect the camper. Frankie cries when he can't go, but he hasn't cleaned his room yet. You're trying to hold your kids more responsible, trying to be a parent again. You take the jar to a window and hold it up to the light. You'll need to buy a calendar today, to do laundry, put away Christmas decorations, to remind Gilly to study for finals. You'll need to put the order in at the Chinese restaurant for the small party you're having tonight: Frogman and Deb, the neighbors up the street. Jimbo is tired of always saying no.

Light refracts through the jar, scattering on the distant wall. The preservative has kept the ovaries remarkably well. They float like uncooked dumplings, this mad detritus of your body.

Frankie comes in and asks you for his breakfast. It's eleven-thirty.

"Can I touch them?" he says, pointing to the jar.

You try to lift him up but your body is so weak. Instead you kneel down and hold the jar in front of his face.

"What are they, Mom?"

"They were inside me," you say. "The doctor took them out. They were making me sick."

Frankie taps at the side of the jar like it's an aquarium. He studies them seriously, trying to imagine how they were once inside you. Like his father, he's always taking things apart and putting them back together.

"Let's go," you say to him.

You begin to dig a hole in the back yard next to the garage. Frankie is reluctant at first, but six inches into the clumpy dirt, he becomes a mad burrower. You and your son dig deeper and deeper. Tailings of dirt and clay form into a hillock against the yellow garage. After an hour, Frankie can sit inside the hole and disappear. After two hours, he can disappear on his tiptoes. You're both covered in dirt. Utterly filthy.

The hole is uneven, and it collapses in places, but it's ten times deeper than need be. You don't believe in ghosts or spirits—most days, you barely believe in God—but you believe in the forces trapped inside that jar, even if you can't say why, and you'll be damned to let them escape.

It takes a fair amount of convincing, but Frankie agrees to go inside and shower before you'll tell him what the hole is for.

You unscrew the top and pour the preservative out first, holding the ovaries inside with the tip of your index finger. They bob up against your skin as the fluid splashes into the dirt. The sensation of your organs against your skin feels electric, like the first touch of a lover's hand.

A small pool of mud forms in the earth. You replace the cap and put the jar down. Then toss dirt onto the mud until it appears dry. The fluid-free jar feels much lighter now. The ovaries bounce around inside. How light they are. They could float away.

Without more than a glance at the jar, you remove the cap again and dump out the ovaries. They plop into the hole. Black dirt quickly adheres to their white tissue. Your stomach heaves. You heap three inches or more of soil on top of them and then three more shovels-full on top of that. Then you drop the jar in. You smash it with the shovel blade and the glass collapses into a thousand shards.

You bury it, all of it, the fluid, your ovaries, the broken glass. You throw shovel after shovel of dirt on top until all of it is back. The hole is still three feet deep.

When it's over, you want to sing, to dance with your dirty feet, like some Pentecostal sinner who has found salvation. But a weird feeling holds you still, a feeling that pinches joy back. When you turn around, its source is made clear.

Gilly stands on the back porch, her hands on her hips, her eyes shiny with tears. It's your own face you see, reconstituted in your daughter. You don't know how much she's seen, but you know instantly it's too much. She must think you've gone irretrievably mad. You wonder how this will affect her later in life. Fucking her up was never part of the plan. But then the joy returns, not in waves, not in spiritual ecstasies this time, but incrementally, like you've awoken from a bad dream and are just now piecing reality back together from the horrible clutches of night terrors.

Gilly chooses the tree—a dwarf orange—and she even holds your hand in the nursery. Frankie picks out a red-barn bird feeder and smiles broadly when you approve of his choice. When Jimbo returns that afternoon, he tells you that he passed on the camper. You reassure him that something else will come along. He asks you about the tree and the bird feeder and the dirt under your nails.

"We needed a project," you say. "Too much sitting around."

In spring, tiny white flowers bloom on the orange tree. Frankie resumes little league practice, Gilly breaks up with her boyfriend but seems happier, and Jimbo buys a small sunfish sailboat in need of new sails and paint. At a follow up appointment, Dr. Rasley discovers and wants to remove a suspicious lymph node from your groin. Jimbo fidgets when the doctor says it should come out now. You hold your husband's hand firmly and smile at him as the worry spreads. You're leaving in the morning for the east coast, but not in the Chevette. You're taking the kids out of school and flying back.

"When we get back," you say. "Not now."

In spite of the grim look in the doctor's eyes, you're certain things will be okay. You squeeze Jimbo's hand tighter, anticipating the long flight across the country with the purest joy. You imagine walking the kids through Boston, then driving away, toward the windswept beauty and rolling, rocky pasturelands of your home. You hope there might still be snow on the ground.

Dr. Rasley begins to explain about new therapies and Jimbo leans in, reassured by the medical evidence and the constantly evolving miracles. But there's no need, anymore, for their reassurances. You block out their voices and imagine the long journey home.

Year Six of Your Seven-Year Sentence: Desert Dandelion

Carrie Moniz

I wake, the wrong man breathing beside me.
Finger your letters under my edge of the bed. On fire
with every word about the yellow flower surviving the yard
outside your window. Only light
from the walled-in square of sky is brighter.
I kiss the wrong man awake, take him into my body
because I have no other place for him.

The Place

Shannon Bates

If I had told you the truth, you never would have come here with me. You never would have trusted me, after all these years. I had to lie. I had no other choice.

I know how much you have wanted to meet your father, to discover who you are, where you came from. I've tried my best to paint you a portrait of a strong, intelligent, and passionate man— one who could only pass down to you the best of genes. There were times when I believed it myself. The stories were becoming true for me, and I actually began to love this man whom I had fabricated from wishes and dreams. I began to miss this person I created to be your father.

I watch you now, as you navigate the stones, avoiding the wobbly ones, to cross the creek without soaking your favorite street shoes. You are agile and graceful, thoughtful and wise. I couldn't have imagined a more perfect son. I follow behind you, more tentatively, occasionally retreating to find a better path. When we both reach the other side, we look back into the forest. The greenness is almost radioactive—vibrant and seeming to grow right before our eyes. The trees and ground cover are much more mature than they were nineteen years ago today. So am I.

I can remember clearly how it looked on that spring day, from this spot just north of the creek. A couple of large stones jutted up and created jets to spill the water back over itself, and there were no dry rocks to keep my feet from getting soaked. My jeans were drenched and heavy, nearly pinning my shoes to the ground. My hair was loose, and I couldn't reach it to keep it out of my eyes.

I told myself that I would never come back here, to this prison of writhing vines and creaking bugs and tugging arms. But it wasn't the forest's choice that I was here on that day and under those circumstances. I figure I owe it to nature to give it another chance.

It's a beautiful place, really. A place where I would love to go to escape, if it hadn't already symbolized capture for me.

You are investigating the landscape, such a lush and verdant terrain, such calmness away from the city. Your hair is getting too long, but you haven't let me cut it in months. *Growing it out,* you say. *No one has short hair these days.* I think it makes you look quite handsome, but I have to be a good mother and say that you should trim it a little to show your face more.

This is the place where I met your father. That is no lie. Out here, in the middle of nowhere, where no one goes to meet anyone else. I can't remember how I ended up here, and why I would have chosen this path, away from all civilization. But this is where I finally lost the race and was tripped up to land face first in a patch of moss. I clawed and I wriggled, but I was not strong enough to regain my footing. I was not even strong enough to keep my jeans—still buttoned and zipped—up on my hips. Burns would show the next day where the jeans were too slim to come down without quite a bit of force. The taste of mud in my mouth was pungent, as the din of the insects hiding in the trees around us joined my screams to sound an alarm to someone, anyone who might be nearby. But it was too late by the time a couple of hikers trotted toward the creek. It was too late for me, and it was too late for your father.

He finally backed off, standing back to admire his work, and I found the adrenaline to heave myself up and hurl my foot toward his sternum. When he pitched back, the creek caught his fall and cradled his head in an arc of stones. As the water ran red, a man and a woman approached, removed their backpacks, and found a cell phone. I squatted, half-naked but completely exposed, and cried until the ambulance came.

I considered telling you about that day—in spite, in truth, or in anger, I'm not sure. I thought about sitting you down here by the creek, brushing your hair back gently to look into your brown eyes, and describing the whole thing. I even practiced how it would go, based on the movie in my head that has been playing over and over for nineteen years. But I like my stories much better. No mud, no blood, no terror. Your father—the one I made up—was a wonderful man who loved you very much. He wanted nothing but the best for you and for me. I've taught you to believe in him as I have, and to be proud of who you are and what you've become. I know I've also taught you not to lie, but I was hoping you'd never have a reason like this one.

You look at me and smile, shaking the hair out of your eyes and spreading your arms wide as if to hug nature. *Thanks for bringing me here*, you say. *It's beautiful. So full of life.*

I smile back and nod my head. *Yes, it is.*

Mother Died On An Exhale

Susan Norton

Over the last few weeks
Mom's body seemed
to get smaller,
turning into itself,
back towards childhood,
as death closed in on her.

Then today,
as I held her hand
like an injured bird
and petted it softly,

she died on an exhale.

The air slipped out
like the *shush*
of someone wanting quiet,
her breath dissolving
into a world of other air.

I pulled back one eye lid
to look inside, now that
she could no longer object.

Her eyes were sealed
in an opaque blue glaze.
Even in death,
she continued to hide
herself from me.

Jade Cove

Janice Coy

I hesitate, shoulders rounded, near the edge of the cliff, close enough to launch a pebble with the toe of my dive boot. The pebble spirals through my shadow and vanishes into the scrub brush twenty feet below. Further down, jagged rocks guard the mouth of a cove with a cobbled beach. The ocean flattens to the horizon, but froths and surges around the rocks with a constant hunger. A strand of black hair whips my cheeks and eyes.

"Ready?" Jakob's warm fingers encompass my chilled ones.

I could blame my tears on the stinging wind and my flailing hair. But more fall at Jakob's touch. I don't bother wiping them. My husband knows I am still grieving my parents. He's been my constant companion since their fatal crash six hellish months ago, putting off business trips that would require nights away. The district attorney is pursuing a long sentence for the drunk driver who killed them; I think of the trial and I foresee the pain stretching endlessly before me like the ocean extending beyond the known horizon. I sigh and turn towards Jakob.

"Sure." My voice sounds more like a question than an answer.

I tighten the straps on my open vest and adjust the scuba tank on my back. Jakob carries my dive weights and fins. A gust of wind sneaks under my sweatshirt. My wetsuit covers my legs, but not my chest—the arms looped together at my waist—and I shiver.

Our trail zigzags to the beach, a thin brown ribbon that hardly seems official. Yet a scarred wooden sign with a yellow arrow identifies it as the entrance to Jade Cove. Two figures appear to be about halfway down the cliff, hiking along the trail.

"I thought we would be the first." Jakob sounds disappointed.

He has planned this jade-hunting excursion so carefully, my first pleasure trip since the accident. I resisted his entreaties to come at first. It wouldn't be right to have fun, to enjoy myself with my husband, while Ma and Ba rotted in their graves.

I finally gave in last week. After Jakob found me on the bottom of a tub full of water, my eyes and lips pressed closed. But all he saw was me under the surface—my floating hair a black shroud—and he jerked my wrist. I emerged spluttering and blinking like a newborn torn from her mother's womb. I pressed my fingers against my eyelids, rubbed the water away. Had the lines that ran along the side of Jakob's nose and made parentheses around his lips always been so prominent? They appeared to have been chiseled deeper.

"Let's go to Jade Cove tomorrow." I stepped out of the tub, my words an appeasement, a half-hearted attempt to reassure my husband that I was returning to life. He pulled me close.

"It's supposed to storm." His clothed chest was warm against mine, the air already chilling my back. I didn't return his embrace. I couldn't tell if my hair had made his cheek damp or if he was crying when we broke apart. He turned away too quickly. Grabbed the towel from its rack, wrapped me in its folds. "We'll go when it's calm." His voice was gruff. "It's best after the storm breaks up the kelp and churns up jade."

We left San Jose well before sunrise, our headlights slicing through the misty fog. The hum of the car's engine and the blast of the heater on my ankles lulled me to sleep, and I rested in the forward motion of the car in a way I hadn't since Jakob threw out the sleeping pills the doctor prescribed. I was jarred awake when Jakob drove into the parking lot, our tires bumping and grinding on gravel. The low sun glanced off the mirror beside me.

Jakob plunges down the trail, and I follow. He has been here before, jade hunting with friends. Free diving to thirty-five, forty feet in search of the stone that could only be found off the Big Sur coast. He says he is breaking me in easy by taking me scuba diving. We can free dive another time.

Ba and I were scuba-certified together. He said it was something he always meant to do. He was just sorry he waited until his fiftieth birthday. Ma said she was not interested in breathing under water; she was perfectly happy reading on the beach.

Moisture pervades the briny air above Jade Cove. I inhale, feeling the fullness of it deep in my lungs. I'm careful on the loose gravel of the trail, but still my foot slides, the bulk of my tank shifts, and I nearly tumble. Jakob steadies me with a hand at my elbow. My legs shake by the time we reach the beach.

We shed our tanks and pile our dive equipment on a flat rock that juts into the water. I balance on one foot, bending my other leg behind me to stretch out my quads. The water pushes small stones back and forth. They clack together with a hollow sound.

"Sometimes you can find jade on the beach," Jakob says. I stretch and Jakob shuffles away, stooping and peering at the ground. I perform several yoga stances before Jakob returns, frowning.

He cradles two stones in his hands.

"No jade," he says. "But here's soapstone." He lifts his left hand. "And this is agate." He shows me the rock in his right hand. "We don't want those."

"I know what to look for," I say. The bluffs protect the beach from the wind, and I peel off my sweatshirt. "I've seen the pieces you have at home."

"They're polished."

I shrug. Jakob tosses the stones aside; one lands with a splintering crack on the beach. The other splats in the water. I tug my wetsuit over my arms, zip the back. The black neoprene feels warm in the spring sun. By the time I tuck my hair into my hood and don my buoyancy vest with its attached tank my armpits are damp.

Jakob hands me my fins. I have never been able to put a name to the color of my husband's eyes, but today, with the ocean roiling behind him, I realize they are sea green. The particular sea green of the water at Jade Cove, a mix of swirling blues, and emeralds and browns.

Nothing like the obsidian black of my parents' or mine.

I remember how the difference excited me when we first met three years ago, and a tiny spark flickers in my heart. A wave slaps against our rock, and I shift my gaze to the water's edge where the stones are black.

I loop my fin straps over my wrist and pick my way across the shallow crevasses of the flat rock. Crouching, sitting, we wait for a break in the sets. Then, one at a time, lower ourselves into the ocean. The first rush of frigid water into my wetsuit shocks me. Goose bumps pimple my skin. I feel more alive than I have in the past six months. I slip on my fins, and kick out into the cove on my back next to Jakob. My heart thumps. My throat feels dry. I'm nervous like every first dive in a new location. I can feel the power of the ocean undulating beneath me, carrying me along like a broken piece of driftwood or rudderless flotsam. The cliffs tower overhead. Jakob nudges me. I don't think to keep my back to the waves, and I swallow a mouthful of salt water. Jakob brushes seaweed off my face, pats my back while I splutter.

"No hurry," he says. "We can wait."

I spit. Nod.

I adjust my mask over my eyes and nose, click on my flashlight and signal a thumbs down for descent.

Kelp ripped into tiny pieces like discarded tissues thickens the water, dropping visibility to about ten feet; we will need to stay close to each other. Jakob motions for me to follow him and we kick deeper. A stout sheephead with a bulging forehead swims in the same direction. Silvery fish appear ghostlike just beyond the reach of my light, probably the lingcod Jakob talked about.

Nervous on the surface, now I enjoy the freedom of the water, the release from gravity and the pressures above, and I fin slowly behind my husband, my hands extended in front as if I were flying. I can feel Ma and Ba in the water's caress, and I imagine them floating just outside the circle of my light like the lingcod. Tears fog the lens of my mask. I can barely see the tip of my husband's black fins. My own light is a misty halo. The light grows brighter, and Jakob is facing me, gesturing for me to clear my mask. I close my eyes and tilt my mask open a crack so a bit of seawater can rinse the fog away. I blow hard through my nose. The water and tears wash out.

A large, rugged shape looms ahead, its edges blurred in the water. Closer inspection reveals the shape as a shallow cave. I follow Jakob inside, not sure what to expect from the dark interior. And I am stunned.

I've been in underwater caves before with Ba. Caves where giant lobsters waved their claws in warning, caves where brilliant turquoise water shimmered like a dive magazine picture, caves we just swam through for the sheer joy of it. But this cave, big enough for two to move about comfortably, is something entirely different.

It glows with subdued green—not everywhere our lights linger, but in spots where I least expect. I'm about to turn my light from a dark crevice and a flicker of color catches my eye, almost like a submerged Emerald City is hidden beneath the plainer rock waiting for someone to scratch the surface and reveal the beauty.

Ba would love this cave; he would be over the rainbow for this cave.

I startle when Jakob touches my shoulder. He shines his light near his face, and his eyes are smiling through the lens of his mask. He moves his hand into the light and circles his thumb and forefinger in the underwater signal for OK. I flash my own OK signal back.

Jakob removes his breathing regulator from his mouth and motions for me to do the same. Our lips touch. His still retain some warmth. My cooler ones tingle. I pull away, and thrust my regulator into my mouth, anxious for the oxygen supply it provides. I train my light on our bubbles, watch as they rise to the top of the cave and burst.

Maneuvering near a wall, Jakob moves his hands over the rocks, jiggling ones that appear loose. I sweep my flashlight in a slow arc around the cave, pausing when a particularly fantastic shade of green catches my eye.

Ba was especially fond of jade and had given several pieces to Ma. Her favorite was a translucent mint-colored good luck symbol she wore on a thin chain. She wore it every day. Even the day of the crash. I didn't know what that meant. What it said about her luck. I thought about burying it with her, but Jakob and the funeral director argued against it. They said I would want something I could hold onto. I draped the necklace over Ma and Ba's picture on the wicker table next to our bed. The jade touching the lower edge of the simple wooden frame, the gold chain a V across their faces.

Jakob hasn't managed to pry a rock loose. I'm glad. I want the cave to stay as it is. Other treasure hunters will come, but I won't witness their efforts to pick apart the cave one rock at a time. I want my memories to be unsullied. Jakob signals for our departure. My light snares a glint of green at the cave's threshold. A rock the size of my index finger sways and rolls with the pitch of the water. I secure it in a pocket of my vest.

We kick along a craggy shelf, mimicking the languid movements of the sheephead that persists in shadowing us. Our flashlights pick out plum-colored anemones and a hermit crab that retreats into its shell.

Jakob probes under the shelf with his light, turning rocks, examining them in his beam. Some he discards, others he tucks into his vest. I'm content to float behind him devoting as little effort as possible to my state of being. Concentrating on the draw and exhale of my breath, the taste of latex balloon that lingers on my tongue.

The tips of my fingers are numb in my gloves, but I'm sorry when the time comes to begin our ascent. Our air supply is low; we must return to the surface.

We follow the slope towards the beach, the sandy bottom giving way to piles upon piles of stones, pushing against each other, scraping and smoothing raw edges.

The underwater surge of the waves pushes me forward only to draw me back again, as if the ocean isn't quite ready to release me from its embrace. The distance between my husband and me grows. The visibility drops this close to the shore. Dense clouds of watery dust are stirred by the waves. Now, I can only see brief glimpses of Jakob's fins. My breathing grows ragged. I struggle to keep up. A sharp stab like a needle jabs my ribs. I double in pain. I press my fingers on the biting spot. My flashlight wobbles in my hand as I peer through the gloom searching for a shark, my breathing shallow, my heart leaping. But there is no dark shadow. No cold eye. No rows of razor teeth. I shine my flashlight on my gloved fingertips sure they must be bloodstained. But my gloves don't glisten with red. My wetsuit is intact: the pain a gas bubble. I fight to calm my breathing.

Jakob's fins are gone, swallowed by the murk. A piece of kelp tissue sticks to the lens of my mask, blinding me. I'm alone. The kelp tissue washes away. Water rushes past my regulator. I swallow a mouthful of ocean; my throat burns from the salt. A powerful surge sucks me down, upending me so my tank scrapes the gyrating rocks. My heart pounds in a crescendo beat. I pant, sucking air that doesn't reach my lungs. I forget I'm a strong swimmer. I forget the surface is within reach. I forget how close I am to the shore. I picture Ma and

Ba, as I have done so many times before, strapped in their seats, the headlights of the car bearing down on them, the brightness clouding their vision. Did Ba even have a chance to turn the wheel? Or did they die in the blink of an eye?

My husband's sea green eyes shimmer in my brain. I remember the pressure of his fingers yanking my wrist, drawing me out of the tub. His arms encircling me. The warmth of his chest. I thrust my arms upwards, my fingers desperate claws. A mighty surge thrusts me forward, almost as if Ma and Ba were shoving me. I kick—hard.

My head breaks the surface. I spit my regulator from my mouth. Gasp. Fill my mouth of air pregnant with the stink of dead kelp and fish. My husband bobs nearby; I choke back a sob of relief. My panic seemed forever, but reality proves only seconds have passed. The waves propel me onto the beach, and I crawl out of the surf past a man gutting a cod. The stones jab my knees even through the protective skin of my wetsuit, but still I crawl until I reach the spot where Jakob removes his fins.

I swing off my tank and recline next to my husband, our shoulders rubbing, my face towards the brilliant sky, my chest heaving. Others shout along the beach, their voices adrift on the wind currents like the sea birds that circle above: wings spread and still.

The rocks shift, move under Jakob. We are silent together.

After a while, my breathing slows and I no longer think about the rise and fall of my chest. I sit up and comb my fingers through the tangle of my hair.

"You look like a mermaid." Jakob smiles. The familiar chip in his right front tooth only makes him more dear to me. "Will you grant your favor to this lowly human? I bring treasures." He retrieves the jade from his vest, offers the stones like a present on the palm of his hand.

One is a light apple green, dented and veined. The other is more blue than green with wavy streaks of black.

"Beautiful." My fingers hover over the pieces, but do not land.

"I found one too," I say.

I reach into my vest. The flash of green I saw underwater has disappeared. A thin layer of white veils the jade—if it truly ever was jade. I had destroyed the rock's beauty, killed its very essence, by bringing it to the surface. With a spurt of anger, I scramble to my feet. I draw back my arm, ready to hurl the rock as far into the ocean as I can. But Jakob stays my hand.

"Let me see."

I drop the ugly stone into Jakob's open palm. It leans against his two pieces like a blemish.

"I picked up the wrong thing." Tears prick my eyes, and I swipe at them. "I guess I don't know jade after all."

Jakob pulls his steel knife from the sheath strapped to his leg. He draws the blade along the surface of the stone. I can't bear to look.

"It didn't scratch," he says. "That's a good sign."

Now, I hold my breath and watch.

Jakob lifts the stone to his mouth and does something completely unexpected. He sticks out his tongue and licks the stone like an ice cream cone. The white layer vanishes, and the green glow I saw underwater is back. The sun seems to bore into the stone, revealing a depth I never knew jade possessed. I gaze into it as if it holds the secrets of the universe. But as soon as Jakob's saliva dries, the white reappears almost as if a thick lace curtain has been drawn.

"It's just a layer of salt. We can wash it off at home." Jakob hands me the rock. "It's a nice piece."

I press my tongue to the stone. A small dab of jade emerges.

"I can polish it," he says. "Make you a pendant."

I'm still staring at the stone when Jakob pulls me close. His warm breath is on my ear. "I love you." His voice is low and fierce.

I lift my face.

For the first time in six months, I feel his kiss. The prickly hairs of his beard scratching my chin, the salt mingling in our mouths: his passion stirring the embers of an emotion I had nearly discarded. I remember Ba placing my hand in Jakob's at our wedding last year, Ma on tip-toe, heels loosed from her fancy shoes, cheek touching my husband's. The cloud of grief lifts a little. I lean into my husband and breathe with the steady thump of his heart. I encircle him with my arms, the jade pressed against his back.

*Interlude**

Judith Barkley

White blouse open at the neck,
sleeves rolled to your elbows,
you walk into the ocean,
surf lapping your feet.
The black and white image belies
arms tanned from summers,
holidays on the sea.
We've seen you on the boat,
sails set, full and taut,
leaning with the wind.
We've seen you on the yacht,
slipping away from paparazzi.

Here, your hands grasp Caroline's.
Arms outstretched,
you swing your daughter,
out and high,
in a circle like an ice dancer.
Caroline flies, her hair brushing the sky.
Your hair flies—
the sea harbors a wind.

Does the wind whisper the sea's sorrows?
No matter.
This moment, wind and sea
love you, love Caroline.

Ocean rolls into sky,
like the sea in your blood
in the blood of your children.
Like water your son's birth will break,
the sea will bear his death, the sky yielding,
and only Caroline to weep, to rage
against the sky, against the sea.

---

*Inspired by Mark Shaw's photograph, "Jacqueline &
Caroline Kennedy, Hyannisport, MA 1959"

Familia Anclada

Denise Kinsley

Do Something About the Children Slain

Dusty blood flows in the road;
red rivers pool in graphics
casting crimson shadows on cement walls:
"Twenty-Four Dead Just South of El Paso"

The supermarket execution
taped off yellow. Her downcast eyes
in remorse, not strong—
just a necessity.

Living in cardboard houses
behind wooden pallet fences.
Unsolved murders
of their sisters and husbands.

Waiting for the maquiladora to boom again.

She cannot cross the desert
with her babies.
The able kids are throwing gang signs
in the alleys littered in crime scenes.

Ay güey

No honest money,
only assimilation to the cartels,
leaving her in warfare.
Prostitution:

normal.

Borders push men back for slaughter.
Time in mourning
to struggle, to pray, to stay

for the factory lineup.
Federal planes flew overhead
during the last soccer game.

Pops' Plane

Lenise Andrade

*P*ops is in the hospital again and they say this time he's not going to make it out. I'm in the waiting room downstairs, watching the sisters and nieces and husbands and kids do the pacing dance. I know I should be talking to them or playing with the kids, but none of it seems to work. I can't imagine being anywhere else today, but I'm still not sure what I'm supposed to do here.

"Angel, come here!" my niece Carol yells at her daughter. It's not Carol's fault. Or Angel's fault. Everyone's tense, and four-year-olds don't know how to act in a waiting room. All Angel knows is that she's around a bunch of people who usually play with her and hold her and make her laugh and today they don't seem to be paying attention to her. Usually when she sees this many of her family in one room, it's someone's birthday or a wedding or Christmas. Angel doesn't know why they're all so serious, so of course she's being funny and playful, running around the chairs or playing peekaboo behind magazines. She just wants someone to smile or laugh. But they keep telling her to shush or to sit still and keep giving her magazines or small toys to play with.

"Angel, *mija*, just play for a little bit, OK?" I whisper in her ear. "Your mom's not mad at you. We just need to be quiet for a little while. I'll take you for a walk later, OK?" She just plays with the toys her mom found in her purse and does a small bouncy nod, not happy but appeased for a while.

"I just can't do this anymore," Carol says to no one in particular. "Seriously, we've been down here too long. When's the next group coming down? Is someone gonna come down and tell us what's going on?" We've been up in Pops' room in shifts. He's been here a few days, seems like weeks though, and the room is pretty small, and there's got to be at least twenty of us here at any given time, so we've been mostly hanging downstairs while a handful go up at a time, the rest of us down here having coffee and watching whatever's on the one small TV mounted up high. We make idle chatter, hug the new ones as they arrive, try to keep the young ones entertained, and go out in shifts to get food and coffee for the ones who won't leave.

I've only been up there a few times so far. Pops was checked in because he passed out in the kitchen and his heart was beating too fast. When the ambulance brought him here, the doctors said he'd had a mild heart attack, which was weird because he never had heart problems before. Mom died twenty years ago from her bad heart, but Pops always seemed like he'd outlive us all. He got diabetes and a mild case of Parkinson's and a few falls here and there—not to mention the numerous times in his youth when he should have died, between bar fights and his time in the war—but here he is, this small man in a worn gown in a crap hospital, the same hospital Mom died in twenty years ago, and it just doesn't seem real. They say his organs are failing and he wouldn't survive any surgeries, really, so the five sisters and we two brothers talked then signed the papers and they say he probably won't make the night. Calls have been made, and those who are up for it have come and those who can't get called with updates, though there hasn't been any change in days. I went up to the room a few times, with a sister here and there, but mainly I've just been trying to stay out of everyone's way. And, frankly, the last hour or two, I can't stop thinking about that damn plane.

Now just to be clear, I'm not one for reality TV or what LA calls news. I watch CNN and read the paper everyday. Back in the day, my sister Mona and I went to rallies against the Vietnam War, and I taught my nieces to be informed and vote and question authority and voice their opinions. So, the junk that passes for "Breaking News" today just doesn't interest me. But if you're stuck in a crap hospital waiting for your father to die, you will end up watching anything on the screen.

See, there's this plane stuck in the air over LA. It was coming in from somewhere on the east coast and planning to land in Burbank. But as they got ready to land, they realized one of the wheels wouldn't come down right. So they circled around Burbank for a bit to see if they could trigger it, but it didn't work. Sometime this morning the news found out about it, and they keep following the plane all over LA, like freaking vultures waiting for it to crash into the streets. So then they tried a bunch of remote computer things to trigger the wheel and it won't give and there's no empty space big enough in Los Angeles where they could crash land and they even dumped a bunch of fuel into the Pacific, hoping the lighter weight would buy them some time. But of course now they have less fuel and the wheel won't come down and so they keep hovering between LAX and Burbank, trying to figure out a way to safely bring the plane down without disturbing too many on board or on land.

And I guess they didn't want to tell the people on board what was up, but before long, all those people who supposedly had their cell phones off heard from friends and family down here watching any station in LA that their plane was "doomed to crash," or whatever splashy phrase those so-called reporters came up with, and then the people on the plane starting calling the stations down here, telling their stories on the air. And all I keep thinking is that this is like some sort of bad movie of the week, but it's real and, though this is the kind of thing I hate, I can't stop watching that plane in the air, waiting for that wheel to come down and make everything all right.

"It's about time," sighs my niece Nicole, as the last bunch of family comes off the elevator into the waiting room. She's the activist one. Not quite the living- -in-a-tree type, but she does work for a nonprofit and has a soft spot for progressive boys who like reading the paper and having a few cold ones while watching late night TV. I helped to raise that girl right. Her ex works for some politician in Boston and I'm not sure who she's dating now, but she tends to keep those things under her sleeve, like a good poker player, until the moment is right. When she was young, I taught her chess and my Pops taught her cards. And my mom bought her plenty of books. We did our best to ready her for the world. "OK," she stands up and announces, "anyone else going up?"

Eyes shift to each other and some busy themselves with kids and nudges and nods and gestures. There's this weird pause, as all those who wanted to go up before now are too busy or too polite, and there's this general "no, you go," and I just shrug at Nicole and get up and figure whoever wants to go up next will go, and I better go up now and talk to Pops a little more, though he can't hear me, or else I'll end up watching more reports about that plane, as if anything is more important than this time here.

Nicole puts her hand on her mom's shoulder and Mona gets up. I love all my sisters, but Mona and I spent many years together growing up, and I think I know her best. She took me to my first protests in Griffith Park, and I moved in with them for a while when Nicole's dad just couldn't stick around. Mona raised Nicole mostly on her own and put herself through school and has done a lot in her time, but things like this just make her crumble, and she's suddenly that thirteen-year-old girl who had to watch the kids back home when Mom went looking for Pops on those nights when pool games turned to hustling, then to bar fights, and then someone had to bail him out of jail. When Nicole was little, she was always very serious, our little grown-up, so sometimes the mother-daughter thing got a little confused. And right now, Mona looks at Nicole like she's some sort of bailiff taking us up to the cells, but she lets out a short exhale and gets in the elevator with the rest of us, as if this may be the last time we deal with whatever trouble Pops has gotten into this time.

It's quiet in the elevator on the way up. Pops is on the eighth floor and this elevator can't seem to go fast enough. In hospitals, people either busy themselves with idle chatter in elevators or they stand in silence. Usually, I'm fine with quiet, prefer it really, but this time it was too much.

"So, does anyone think that plane's gonna crash?" I ask. Nicole half turns her head my way and just glares. We ride up the rest of the way in silence.

Pops looks so skinny and light in the bed, like I could just pick him up and toss him around. Not that I would. The man's eighty-seven and completely out of it, but I remember a time when just the raising of his voice could make me pee my pants. I mean, it was a different time back then, and the man did what he could with seven kids in East LA. And sometimes we deserved to get beat. We acted up, snuck out of the house, lied, smoked, drank, and got in fights, often with each other. We weren't always perfect. And sometimes neither was he. But that old man tried.

Once I got busted ditching school, and when mom told him what I had done, he chased me around the kitchen table. He got close enough to kick me in the butt, but I was just a step ahead of him and, when he went to kick me and got nothing but air, he ended up flat on his ass. This caused my brother and sisters, who had been watching from the living room, to burst out laughing, which made Pops even more pissed, which meant I was now in even more trouble. I got an even harder kick when he finally caught me, but it was worth it though, because that's still one of my favorite memories of him.

Another time, when I was very little, maybe five or six, I remember hearing people yelling outside. I remember going to the window and seeing Pops and some guy yelling in the street. The guy said Pops had cheated him and he was going to get what he deserved. The guy had to be a foot taller than Pops and definitely wider, but Pops got right in his face and yelled how dare he come to his house and threaten him and his family. Then he grabbed the guy by the wrist and brought him to his knees and began punching and kicking him, pummeling the guy against the sidewalk. Years later, I thought I had made this up but when I asked about it, Mona said she remembered that night too and she had thought that Pops was going to kill the guy for coming to the house. That's when I knew what Pops was capable of and, even when he wasn't always right, I knew he'd do what he could to take care of us.

Mona and Nicole are busy cleaning up Pops. Where the tubes in his arm are stuck in, there's some dried blood, and they seem to think his oxygen mask is too tight. True, when they pull it back, he does have dents in his face, but I want to tell them it needs to be tight so he can get air and his old skin doesn't bounce back like it used to, but I just let them fuss. It gives them something to do. Mona takes the mask off for a minute, because it looks tight, she says, but really I think she just wants to see his whole face without any hospital things in the way. They rearrange his pillows and straighten up his gown, all the while talking to him and telling him who's in the lobby and how everyone's here and all that. He's fast asleep, or whatever you call it, but they are sure he can hear them. Mona's husband hands them supplies as they ask for it, washcloths and tissues and even another rosary. Pops must have twenty freaking crosses or rosaries on him, around each wrist, three around his neck, and I think I even see one tucked under his shoulder. I mean, I know we're Catholic, but this is a little much, and I really can't see how it's going to help at this point, but I guess everyone is just doing what they can.

I sit on one of the chairs in the back and watch his chest rise and fall. His breaths are short and uneven. Even though he's out cold, I can hear his voice going "Ay, alright already, *deja me*, leave me alone." He hated being fussed over. Maybe with mom he would have let some of this slide, but this was his daughter and his granddaughter, and in his eyes, he was supposed to take care of them, not the other way around.

"What's this?" Nicole pulls back a bit of his gown down around his left shoulder. "MB? What's that stand for?"

"It's not MB," Mona tells her. "It's MR, for Maria Rodriguez. It's your grandma's initials."

"Seriously? Grandpa has a tattoo? He totally yelled at me when I got mine. What a hypocrite!" Nicole wants to be pissed but she also looks like she might laugh any minute.

"Well, he thought tattoos looked cheap on women," Mona explains. "He didn't want his granddaughter looking like a tramp." They both try not to laugh but a little chuckle finds its way through.

Behind where Mona's husband stands is another small TV mounted on the wall. The sound's down, but it looks like they have a plan for the plane. They cleared a bunch of runways at LAX and were going to try a crash landing. I guess they figure, if the plane can't stop, it would just slide into the ocean and they could rescue people from there. It seems like a crap plan to me, but I guess it was all they had. The ticker at the bottom keeps repeating the plan over and over while the plane coasts over the airport and then a bit over the water, turning and turning in large circles, waiting to be told what to do next.

The door opens and my other sister, Diana, comes in, wheeling our Tia Rosa in. That woman has been using a walker or a cane for as long as I can remember, and I guess she finally upgraded to a chair. I can't even remember the last time I saw her. She rarely leaves the house anymore, so I guess that's why Diana brought her up, out of turn and over our visitor limit. They wheel her close to Pops, as close as possible with the chair and all. Mona and Diana lift her up a bit, so she can lean in to Pops. He's looking a little more pale than before, like I can almost see through his skin, it's so pale. Tia Rosa prays a bit in Spanish over him, asking God to help him find his way, whether it is here or with Him. Mona and Diana and Nicole pass worried looks at each other but I think this lady's got the right idea. Everyone's been fussing and talking about tubes and I know they signed a do-not-resuscitate order, but they're still acting like something else can be done. One of the nurses told them his organs are failing, and I was standing right there when she said it, but it was like my sisters never heard it. Tia Rosa keeps talking to him in Spanish, telling him not to worry, *no te preocupes*, that his family is strong and together and he's done a great job with us, but now it's time to go home, to go be with mom and his brothers and family up there. And I swear I see him swallow, and his mouth parts a bit like he's going to say something, but all that comes out is air.

That's when I notice the plane again. But now it looks like it's flying straight towards something, slowly lowering, I guess ready to attempt the landing. And it seems too soon, like maybe there should be another hour of hovering or another plan, but here it is landing, and it seems like it's going slower than any plane should, and they bring the wheels down, and that front one does come down, but not all the way, and it still doesn't look sturdy enough for this. The plane reaches the runway and comes down on its back wheels first, very slow and even, and I feel myself hold my breath and wait to see the front of the plane come down. And almost in slow motion, the nose of the plane tilts downward, and that cockeyed wheel hits the asphalt. Sparks and smoke shoot out of where the wheel is, but the plane is still moving, slowing down but moving steadily forward. And after what seems like forever, the plane does stop and it lands safely. Smoke is coming out from where the tire was shredded but no fire has started. They are yards from the edge of the runway, where it would have hit the ocean, but the plane has landed and I imagine everyone on it is safe.

I turn to the others to see if they watched it too, and that's when I notice that Mona is crying big heaving sobs onto Pops' chest. Her husband has his hand on her back, doing his best to comfort her.

Diana and Nicole are rubbing Pops' head, and I can't tell if they're praying or talking to him, but they're crying too and they suddenly look so tired. Tia Rosa has sat back in her chair, hunched over a rosary, praying, with one hand on Pops' leg.

And that's when I notice the monitor has that flat line they talk about. I guess I thought it would make a sound or warn us or something, but it's just flat and still and the room is very quiet, except for the quiet sobs and mumbling of prayers and words of comfort. In just a few seconds, Pops is gone and I missed it. I want to tell him something, let him know I was there and I care, and I want to move closer to the bed, but I can't move my legs and I just stare at his face. But all the color is already gone from his face and he isn't the man I remember, just a body already, and I feel bad but I think I should feel worse. My sisters and niece are a wreck, and I think of all the people downstairs and having to go down there and tell him it's over, that Pops is gone, but all I can do is stand there and wait, wait for the next step.

And that's when he takes my hand. I look to my right, and there's the man I know. All six feet of him, tall and proud and dark and fierce. Pops is standing right next to me, as calm as can be. He looks at the rest of them, crying and praying and hugging each other. He gives a long sigh, squeezes my hand once, and says to me, "It's okay, *mijo*, they'll be fine. I'm ready. It's time for us to go." And so we turn and I am ready to go too, because now I have something to do.

Prophetess

Nancy Sandweiss

A ghostly chorus lines the sidewalk leading to the opera hall.
Passing by, I read a dark libretto in scruffy beards, bloodshot eyes,
ragged army surplus; in rusty carts stuffed with bulging knapsacks
weathered tarps.

A solitary man spreads bedroll, boxes, cardboard shelter
by an intersection, close enough to feel the rush of cars, hear
the squeal of brakes. Some seek communal safety, their blankets
touching; others stake claim to covered doorways.

They could be actors in a mythic hellish drama. Cassandra herself
slumps on a curb, electric hair framing a silent shriek.

Why Are the Blinds Closed?

Brian Peyton Joyner

"Why are the blinds closed?" Momma asks.

Strolling into the den after a night at the movies with my friend Austin, I don't expect an inquisition about blinds. I expect to find my parents sitting on opposite sides of the loveseat watching TV. Her question squeezes my stomach so tight I feel popcorn and co-cola pushing up to the back of my throat.

Momma's on the edge of the couch, twisting and pulling at the under-loop curl of her brown helmet hair. Dad's beside her, rubbing his lips with his thumb and pointer finger. I stand in the doorway, a little fearful of entering.

Momma repeats her question. "Ben, why are the blinds closed?" The pencil thin eyebrows she draws on every morning meet in the middle, and horizontal lines cross her brow much like the blinds should be.

I could deny that I was the one to close the blinds, but Momma's point is the "why" not the "who." Blinds open and close. That's what they do when you twist the wooden dowel. But we never close those blinds in the den. Not even when Momma or I dust them.

"I was showing Austin how the blinds match the cherry paneling," I say, keeping my eyes wide open. Momma and I heard on NPR last week that people blink a lot when they're lying. Part of what I was telling them was the truth. It was what I told Austin when I closed the blinds.

Momma mumbles what I just said. "The blinds match the cherry paneling." She looks at Dad letting him know it's his turn to interrogate me. He's chewing on his upper lip. He touches her knee and turns to her. I notice the first gray in his light brown hair. He clears his throat and coughs.

I stare at Dad and Momma and then say, "Also, Austin and I were watching TV for a bit before we left. Closing the blinds reduces the glare."

Don't blink.

Dad clears his throat again and then whispers to Momma, "I need something to drink." He stands up and when he walks past me, he squeezes my elbow. It's his way of letting me know I'm on my own.

Momma and I are in a duel, at ten paces, and we've got our arms down by our sides, hands hovering over our pistols. I know she can see my heart thumping in my chest and sweat balls forming on my forehead. Momma draws first.

"What's going on with y'all?" she asks. "You and Austin?" The way she says his name, it's almost like she's saying "Satan."

I take a deep breath in and out through my nose to let her know that I'm irritated by this line of questioning. "Nothing, Momma." Criminals flee the scene of a crime so I decide I'd better stay and act like nothing's happened.

Momma pats the sofa cushion beside her, but I don't take my usual place in the middle of the loveseat. I plop down in the leather wingback chair in front of the fireplace where just last weekend I posed for prom pictures with my girlfriend. Already, Momma has put a photo of us on the mantle.

"You like the picture?" Momma asks. She's studying me as I sit there, blinking her eyes real fast like she's processing images, like if she watches each move I make, she'll figure it all out.

I cross and uncross my legs trying to think how a straight guy would sit, and then choose to interpret her question as one about the movie picture Austin and I just saw. "*Steel Magnolias* was even better than *Driving Miss Daisy*. Y'all gone really love it. The plot and acting were amazing."

Momma grabs the back of her hair with her fist and then pulls at it. "I'm talking about the photo of you and Becca."

My left knee bounces up and down. I can't stop it so I stand up and grab the photo. In the pic, I'm resting my hand on Becca's shoulder. The teal blue color of my cummerbund and bow tie look worse in the photo than I remember. Becca sits up real straight in the chair and pushes out the A-cup boobs I've felt twice through her shirt. I didn't really want to feel her boobs, but after a week of being teased at school about never making it to second base, I decided to give them a squeeze. Then at least, I could talk about how boobs felt without blinking.

In the photo, Becca folds her arms left across right, showing the wrist corsage the florist helped me pick out. He was a high school classmate of my parents and according to my Momma was "that way" even in high school.

"Nice frame," I say to my Momma. "Is it real silver?"

"Plated," she says. Her eyebrows meet in the middle again, and I think about how we could all be on the couch watching a movie about a kid with cancer or something if only I hadn't closed the blinds. But if my parents came home early from their Sunday school class potluck, I didn't want them to see me and Austin using the loveseat for its original purpose.

I put the photo of me and Becca back on the mantle and move it forwards and backwards, left way and right way, trying to get it back to its original spot. Momma starts tugging at her hair again, then flattens it in the back so it doesn't stick out. I'm aware of the silence between us as the moments pass. From the kitchen, the sound of ice cubes dropping into a crystal tumbler decides the final position of the photo. Dad walks back into the den with a whiskey. His first drink in 59 days.

I forget all about Austin, the blinds, prom pictures and movies. I'm driving my Dad to drink, and I want to shout "Stop!" I wanna knock the drink out of his hand and answer Momma's question. Tell them what they wanna hear.

But they don't wanna know the truth.

So I'm silent.

We're all silent.

My heart beats faster, blood whooshes past my eardrums and my cheeks get warm. I blink and lick my lips. I can still taste Austin's menthol-flavored Blistex.

Dad looks at me and Momma with one eyebrow raised, almost a dare for us to say anything. He takes up the other wingback chair. Dad's gray-green eyes, the same color as mine, are red and puffy. I wonder if this is his first drink tonight or if he's been crying. From Momma's face, she's shocked to see he's got whiskey. Her eyes widen. Her eyebrows angle up and down. The crystal tumbler touches Dad's lips. He takes a sip.

I think about what my father's sixty-day chip would have looked like. Definitely gold-colored. Probably real metal. Not like the plastic silver-colored chip he'd gotten at day thirty. But tomorrow, when he skips evening church service to go to AA, he'll have to stand up and say, "I'm Gene, I'm an alcoholic and my last drink was yesterday."

Momma looks back and forth at me. At Dad. "Something you wanna tell us, Ben?" she asks.

It's a question I wish I could answer. I love Becca. Much more so than I like Austin, but when I'm lying in bed at night, it's him I think about, not her.

Dad gulps down half the glass of whiskey and sets the tumbler directly on the cherrywood coffee table. Momma stands up, tugs at the bottom of her blouse, walks over, and picks up Dad's glass. She wipes up the wet ring with her sleeve and sets the tumbler on a coaster. She sits on the coffee table right in front of me so that her bony knee presses sharp against mine. She leans in, and I see the thin lines under her brown eyes. Her mascara hasn't been running. Her mascara is clumped the same way as when she left that evening. "Well?" she says.

A lifetime in this family has equipped me to turn off my emotions and detach. I know I'm not gonna tell them about Austin, and I'm not afraid of her questioning anymore. I take a wad of crumpled Kleenex from my pocket. At the movie, Austin handed a few to me during the graveside scene.

I shift in the chair and lean back until I don't feel her sharp knee. "Take a tissue when y'all go see *Steel Magnolias.* I cried like a girl when Julia Roberts died." I dab at my eyes like I'd done during the movie but smell Austin's Polo cologne on the Kleenex. My face burns red hot. The flames of hell lick at my cheeks.

"You cried when Julia Roberts died," Momma says, but not in a question-y way. Her voice is flat at the end. Dad sighs and reaches for the tumbler with the rest of the alcohol, but Momma slides it to the other side of the table. She slaps my knee. Not hard, but like she used to do when I was a kid standing in line at the grocery store and

I'd reach out for a candy bar she didn't want me to have. This pop doesn't hurt. Just makes a sound.

At the back of my throat, I taste the oily, butter flavor of movie popcorn. I swallow it down without breaking my focus.

"You know your Dad and I wanted to see that movie next weekend," Momma says. "How dare you spoil the ending?" She picks up Dad's drink and then goes into the kitchen. I hear the clink of the ice as she pours the drink down the sink. I look at my father, but he won't look at me. I want to tell him I'm sorry, but I can't think what I would apologize for.

I think about calling Austin and telling him about everything, but that might be the smoking gun they're trying to find at this crime scene, so I smell the Kleenex one last time and then shove it back into my pocket.

Dad stares at the coaster on the table and licks his lips, savoring the last drops of whiskey.

I cut on the TV and change the channel to Wheel of Fortune. At first, each puzzle is just blank spaces, but then after Vanna White turns around one letter and then another, eventually, I can solve the puzzle. I realize closing the blinds was the letter my parents needed. I just wonder if they were ready to solve the puzzle.

The next day is Sunday, and when Momma and I get home from worship service, Dad is in the den, sitting on the loveseat, watching TV. On the coaster, on the coffee table in front of him, is a large coin, about the size of a half-dollar.

It's gold and has the number 60 on it.

Momma sits down beside him on the other side of the loveseat. She notices the AA chip. Her pencil eyebrows separate as she smiles. "Good job, Hun," she says to him, and then looks at me. She's waiting for me to say something. To congratulate him too. Her eyebrows angle down and up.

The room starts to spin. I'm a fly seeing little flecks of the scene. Momma's sunshine-yellow Sunday church dress. The thin tint of gray to Dad's hair. The silver of the frame. My electric blue cummerbund. Becca's white orchid wrist corsage. I'm tired of this performance. I don't want to participate anymore. I wanna go upstairs and change out of my church clothes. Take this tie off and put on sweat pants. I have a paper to finish, and I need to maintain my GPA.

But Momma pats the cushion area beside her. She scooches over, away from Dad, to make room for me to squeeze between them.

So I squeeze.

The three of us on the loveseat. The smell of Momma's Jean Nate Cologne and of cigarette smoke from Dad. He doesn't smoke, but the folks at AA do, so it's on his clothes. Dad turns to me, "I closed the blinds. Lot less glare on the TV."

Momma nods and then we watch the rest of the program. It's a Hallmark movie. One where Dad and I will cry at the end while Momma plays critic, pointing out the flaws in the plot while praising the actors.

Silent Movie

Eber Lambert

You cast me in little pieces:

I'm a scattered, nervous film,
a blank corrugated soul
whispering confetti.
I settle as dust, a fleeting mosaic,
a flickering mood.
My darkened silhouette blurs
against your scribbled twilight.

I hold you like a silent movie;
our crepe luminescence
miming hand-printed dialog
from stop-action lips,
mottled phrases uttered in
fading ornate fonts.

Time walks slightly faster
when a scripted affair plays
barrelhouse piano to an empty theatre.

I wend away a finished reel;
non-causal pratfalls, an uncut sequel:
Our Sisyphean love.

My fingertips roll across your body
like repelling magnets;
a few precious frames added
unfocused creation,
spliced with blue screen tricks and clever placards.
The remake will come through your lens:
Any tomorrow will do.

You'll recollect me in little pieces.

October Sun: Chapter 17

Corinne Goria

*T*he sun is nearly perennial in Tzintzuntzan due to its location near the equator. Bald light floods the flatlands as soon as the sun rounds the rim of the earth. It ascends rapidly, hovering and staring hotly on roofs and skulls until evening when, without cooling, it slips again silently, without demur, behind the earth's shoulder.

It is midday.

Maria is folding damp clothes on the bed in her mother's house. It is the same bed that has always been there. Pablo is sleeping, naked except for his cloth diaper, curled like a finger on the bed. Adriana is outside in the kitchen, grinding corn into a sandy paste for tortillas. Their rooster wanders about the ground near Adriana's feet, pecking up stray kernels. The mother of Maria and Adriana is working in the tomato harvest today. The house is quiet.

Maria smooths out the stiff creases made by hanging and stacks the sheets and skirts and T-shirts on the bed next to her baby. She gets up to retrieve the remaining clothes strung up outside, but a loud, splintering knock stops her. She stops by the bed. She listens. The faint moan of the corn grinder has stopped and it is silent.

Bang, bang, bang. This time flatter, rattling the entire door in its frame. Maria thanks God the door has been latched, but the latch is also wooden—a small pivoting hook carved from the same tree that will hold up no better than the door.

Adriana creeps into the bedroom. "It's him," she says. Adriana goes to the door leading to the laundry line and the chicken yard and shuts it quietly, latching it. She does the same with the door separating the bedroom from the main room. The front wall bangs loudly again and there is a call. "Maria, get out here. It's time to go."

Adriana and Maria look around the room. The bed is in the far corner against the wall. There is a small table next to the bed, a stack of shelves made with concrete bricks and wooden planks for clothes sitting opposite the bed, a hammock hanging near the door to the chicken yard, and two of their four chickens, standing outside the door, twisting their heads with curiosity in the hot gray air. Pablo sleeps tightly among the sheets and skirts on the bed. The pounding again, cut short. A rustling of banana leaves outside. He was coming around to the back door. Adriana looks at Pablo. Maria begins to shake.

"Under the bed. With the clothes. I'll say you're working with Mama."

"What about Pablo?" Maria whispers.

"Him, too."

Maria carefully lifts sleeping Pablo. She sets him on the sheet Adriana has placed on the ground. They slide him under the bed without disturbing his position.

The door leading to the chicken yard slams in its latch. Crash, crash, crash. "Maria! Now!" she hears.

Maria gets on her stomach and writhes like a snake under the bed. Adriana pushes the folded sheets and clothes around them so all that can be seen from the outside are stacks of pale yellowed sheets and faded colored skirts, folded. In the dark damp under the bed, Maria slides her hand up, splaying it carefully over Pablo's side-turned face. Maria summons God in her mind.

Adriana steps quietly to the other room, leaving the door to the bedroom slightly ajar. Maria hears the rooster squawk outside. She must have gone back to the kitchen, Maria thinks. Maria's face is turned toward Pablo, one cheek pressed to the crumbling dirt pack and the other brushed by the old mattress. The air is humid, thick with mildew from the sheets stuffed around them and from the sweat pouring off of Maria's face. She struggles to get her nose above it for more oxygen. Maria's chest is quaking with the thumping of her blood and, despite the heat, shivers are traveling up and down her body like waves in a washtub. She feels her groin contract and release. She might urinate. She hears voices.

The voices move into the main room, along with boot steps on the dirt pack. Her husband, Juan Carlos, and Adriana.

"You can look around for yourself. She's not here. She went with Mama to harvest tamarind. At the Perez ranch. You can look for her there if you want."

"No esta a cosechando tamarindo, vaca. La cosecha se acabo hace un mes. Donde esta?"

Maria feels the deep vibrations of his voice as thick and heavy as the steamed air draping her nostrils under the bed. Maria feels the vibrations of his voice through the floor and through her chest, as though it is her own internal voice, as though it is God. She shudders violently and Pablo's small face turns under her hand. She hears steps approaching and the interior door of the bedroom slam against the wooden boards of the wall. A warmth gushes into her thighs, and a liquid crawls up into her nasal cavity. She hears her husband kicking over the shelves, boards and bricks clattering, hears him open the door to the chicken yard, take several steps out and then pause. Pablo stirs. In the dark, humid cocoon under the bed, where light crept low through the pale, piled sheets and not at all through the walls, Maria feels Juan Carlos's presence as close as her own. As close as God's.

Pablo moves his head back and forth silently, as though to shake off Maria's hand. Maria lifts her hand from his face slightly then tightens it over his nose and mouth. Juan Carlos is standing at the foot of the bed. Maria is stone stiff, and then, from her chest, she feels a tremor. She begins to smile. Her face has mistaken this hiding with a game. She tries to stifle the giggles that begin to creep up through her arms, neck, and face, horrified at the mistake, the betrayal, her body has made.

Pablo continues writhing his face beneath her grip but it is Maria who is making small whimpers now. She hears Adriana trying to coax Juan Carlos into the main room and hears Juan Carlos speechlessly bend down by the bed and begin to pull the sheets and skirts from underneath. Light and air rush back in around Maria and Pablo and soon Maria feels her ankles grabbed and her body being dragged from its damp warmth across the granulated floor into the middle of the room. Juan Carlos lifts her up completely by her ankles and she feels, briefly, as a child swung upside down. He flings her head first out the open door, her cheek landing on the concrete bricks, chickens flapping hurriedly away.

Loneliness as a Paper Bag

Douglas Payne

Alone on a park bench,
I hold the brown bag
that coddles my cancers.

A dry turkey sandwich
or the head of a Greek god
sawed off the stone body,
to pull it out and just chew
at the thoughts.

Perhaps a raw pint:
like jazz cooking cold winter air,
sultry notes of smoke and honey;
like those springtime girls running past,
their taste of sweet grass and apathy.

Crumpled rejoinders
that most toss away:
like Marx mincing Hegel,
or God as a bum
converting street corners
in old dancing shoes,

bringing it all back homeless.

Things Could Be Worse

Jim Brega

*H*ow'm I doin'? I'm feeling pretty good today, actually. Thanks for asking. I spend a lot of time just sitting around these days, though. I like these steps made out of poured concrete that lead up to the house and give me a good view of the street, and I spend most of the day sitting here and watching people go by. The steps aren't too uncomfortable, and there's no room for a chair or anything, so I take what I can get. Everyone says the steps look pretty natural—like stones or rocks, I guess—probably the way things at Disneyland look natural, if you catch my drift. That's what people say, anyway. I've never been, so I don't know.

I used to get around a lot more, especially before I moved here. I was very long and lean back then, if you can believe it. Not a fat slob like I am now. I was quite a gymnast, really. Not a pro or anything; it wasn't like I competed in any of your standard events, like parallel bars or rings or things like that. But I used to live near the forest, so I could do a lot of mountain climbing—climbing of all types, basically. That's what I used to do. Eventually, after I moved here, I just lost interest; it got repetitive. You know how that goes. You start out doing something, you're having a good time, and one day you wake up and think, screw it, I don't feel like doing anything today, and that's it: the beginning of the end. Tomorrow maybe you do it or not, the next day it's less likely that you do it, and before long you're never doing it. That's life.

I used to have a friend who lived with me here; his name was Raff. Well, he was more than a friend, if you catch my meaning—wink, wink. Some people don't like to hear about that kind of stuff, much less see it, but he was a good friend and I miss him a lot. He was fun—funny, you know? Like, one thing he used to do was mimic people, their expressions and everything; they would stare at him like they were trying to figure out what was going on. Then they'd say, "Are you mimicking me?" and get kind of pissed. So everyone would be staring at him, and he would be staring back, mimicking them, and I'd be trying not to laugh and give it away.

Yeah, he was always ready with a joke or a trick, though he could have his dark moods, too—very dark. No, I mean it! Seriously! He would scream, kick things sometimes; he could destroy almost anything with a single kick when he was angry. He was kind of small and would get pissed off if he heard someone say something like "short stuff" or, worst of all, "pygmy." Well, who wouldn't? But that's the way it goes. Other times he was as sweet as could be, and quite a hedonist, if I have that word right; that's what people would call him, anyway. He could lie stretched out in the sun for hours, barely moving a muscle, perfectly happy.

He was sick when he moved in here, though people didn't realize it. It was funny, you know—not "ha-ha" funny, but weird. Sad—because his name means "healed by God," but he wasn't. God didn't come into it at all; if he had, Raff would still be here, because Raff is basically a good guy—*was* basically a good guy. So, now I don't believe in gods.

I knew about him being sick, and it made all the fun we had together a little sad, too. When he got sicker, people started to notice and talk about it. Like the doctors would call him "lethartic" or something like that. He used to talk about it himself; he used to worry that I would get sick just from being around him, but I never did. He would worry about what it would be like for me when he had to leave. It was hard for me to listen because I didn't want to think about what I would do if he wasn't here. Who would I play around with? Who would tell me jokes? It's been twenty years since he was taken away in the middle of the night; I didn't even realize he was gone until morning. I still think about him almost every day. I don't know if you ever lost someone you loved, but I loved Raff and then I lost him and it sucks, man. It really sucks.

So, I still go on here, a little slower than I used to be, a little more white in the hair, a little less running around, a little less heave-ho, if you know what I mean. They try to tell you that things get better as you get older, but I think things get bitter. Did you catch that? I just wanted to show you I can make a joke too. Okay, I can see you're not laughing; I guess it wasn't that funny.

Maybe you're wondering why I don't make friends with the neighbors. Well, the place on one side is empty, you can see that;

there's a lot of work going on over there lately so maybe somebody new is moving in. The guy on the other side isn't very friendly—a real baboon, if you catch my drift. But at least most of the folks on the street are smart enough to be reasonably close to the top of the food chain—ha ha! There used to be a tour bus that ran by here—no, really! Right past my front steps. There was even a bus stop right in front of the place next door. It hasn't been by for awhile, maybe a couple of years. But this is still a good place to just sit a little and watch the world go by. Things could be worse.

You start to notice stuff, though. For example, kids these days don't seem as polite or as well behaved as they used to be; some of them absolutely belong in a zoo! Sometimes they yell names at me I don't even understand, but I can tell they're not nice. They'll throw junk at me when their parents aren't looking—things they pick up from the street! Pebbles, drink cups, stale hot dog buns. I mean, if you're going to throw a bun at least give me a little hot dog with it! See, there I tried again. I guess you're really not in a laughing mood today.

Anyway, these kids—the simple truth is I don't have the energy to react anymore. I just sit here and think to myself, fuck you, fuck you, some day you're going to be old and I hope some snotty-nosed little sub-primate dumps a whole garbage can on you, you little twerp, but I don't say anything. In a way I don't want people to notice me, you know? Well, present company excluded, of course! But if other folks noticed me, they might think something was wrong. Maybe I'm too old, getting a little lethartic myself or something—and then they'd take me away, too. At other times I think it might not be too bad; if they took me away, I might find Raff again.

So, there's not much to distract me other than the people walking by. Some stop for a conversation, like you, but it's a little one-sided, if you can believe it—ha ha! I think most folks really can't be bothered to try to figure me out. To be honest, I'm not even sure I'm gettin' through to you right now. Yeah, I mean you! Who do you think I've been talking to all this time? STOP! I've got to finish telling you something!

Okay, so I know a lot of people don't get where I'm coming from, don't understand what I'm saying; I put it down to being of different generations or something. Anyway, more and more often I just keep my mouth shut, which makes it hard to make new friends. I'm glad people still come by though; it gives me something to do, something to watch. Thanks, by the way—I appreciate it! But that's as far as things go, these days: watching. Not many people want anything to do with a fat old geezer like me anymore. I know I don't do much grooming, and I probably stink, even though I can't smell anything myself. It's not like anybody could get close to me if they wanted to, anyway. There's always some kind of barrier between us. That's what I wanted to talk to you about. Sometimes I get the feeling that the people walking by know something about me that I don't, as weird as that sounds. Or maybe it's because of the different generations, like I said; or maybe it's their bad manners, or maybe it's just me, just because I'm sad a lot of the time. But being alone here, it's not good. No good at all.

Anyway. So here's the question. This is what I wanted to ask you. There's one thing that's bothered me, all the years I've been living here. There's this sign fastened to my front fence I've never seen, never been able to read. No, really—I can't read. I know, you're surprised. So people come by, and they stare and stare at this sign, and then everyone always says the same thing, over and over: Bonobo, Central Africa. What the hell does that mean?

Investments

Linda Hutchison

slender white pen
Marriot Resort
Newport, left
in my car
raining
you write
down names
of stocks
I should buy
no load
you call them
as I watch
the rain
tiny rivers
separate and weightless
on the other side
of the glass

Winter, Nebraska

Megan Elliot

O n the fifth anniversary you drive out to the old place. You steer the car over the dirty, half-plowed roads, taking the long way around, past the Pearson farm, since the bridge over the creek washed out in one of those big July thunderstorms, two, maybe three years back. These roads are so familiar you could drive them in your sleep, and at times you feel you must have. In those long-ago seasons you would do eighty miles an hour in a straight line across three counties and be back in bed before sunrise, praying that in the morning you'd make it to the shower before someone smelled the alcohol on your breath or the scent of your new boyfriend's cheap cologne on your skin. Those times seem like a dream to you now, hazy and cobwebbed, a series of events with no logical connection to the present.

The lane to the yard is a long tunnel, a thin layer of snow on the floor, the walls and ceiling made of the curling trunks and limbs of dying elm trees. You leave the car on the side of the road and walk up the drive, propelled by something beyond your control, a primal need to return to the scene of the disaster. A pile of scarred and rotted planks, damp under the snow, sits where the house once stood, and in your mind you pick up these pieces, rebuilding so you can see things as they were before: the gray weathered boards, the sagging front porch, a bright red curtain at the kitchen window, fluttering in the hot summer breeze.

On those thick August nights you used to crawl out your bedroom window and lie on the porch roof, smoke cigarettes, and watch stars blink in the inky sky. Back then you dreamed of going places—New York, Machu Picchu, Rome—but not anymore. Now you lie awake and consider the gas bill, your bank account, new brakes for the old car. Sometimes you think not of summer but of winter and that last cigarette smoked in the January darkness, the one you were sure you put out, and the memory of it seeps into your dreams. When that happens, you often wake with a start, and you have to get out of bed and search for the smoke you swear you sensed in your sleep. The acrid smell has never quite gone away, and you live with it like you live with the memory of the crackling flames.

In the cold half-dawn five years ago, you stood barefoot in the snow wearing a faded flannel nightgown, watching your home burn, sucking your breath down in ragged gasps to dull the pain. Today, you hug your arms to your chest, tracing the rough pattern of your skin through the thin sweater you always wear to hide the scars.

I never returned

Seretta Martin

to that chicken coop on the river bank in India Neck
where my son and I were poor and cold
in three rooms with a ventilator stove, were we sometimes
ate mac & cheese for a week, and his school lunches
were my employee meals from the Summit House.
Yet our Cadillac Sedan de Ville, a lover's gift, boasted
leather interior the color of chocolate, and when we pulled up
in front of the laundromat, my son's pinky on that button
in the glove box made the trunk fly open—
We would unload our clothes baskets from that classy car
into the coin-op as small-town women gossiped and glared,
their tongues spinning lies like the tumble of scorched jeans
in a hot drier. But we were rich with our restaurant
and Dunkin Donut friends who sparked our lives
like firecrackers at Branford Point Park, their help and
my waitress tips keeping us from sinking into welfare checks.
I bought a black & white TV on layaway, and it took
two years to pay off the rocking chair. My son played
on the banks of the Connecticut River the day
his father kidnapped him for the third time. That night,
drinking myself into a stupor, I thought I heard someone
at the door and kept my hand on a butcher knife under the pillow.
I can still hear the mating call of Canadian geese on the marsh.
Across the water, the train moans past the wire mill
where young men's teeth corrode from chemical fumes.
In the junkyard, our luxury car must be rusting away, guarded
by Slippers, then a puppy from our Trusty's only litter. Surely
the blue freedom paint is gone. I never returned to that cottage
where I came close to madness, but didn't break. Yet I know
the odor of fish and lilac loiters at low tide, and the tire swing
sways empty in the snow.

Contributors

Lenise Andrade is a Los Angeles native and graduate of the University of Southern California. She uses her English degree and customer service experience to fundraise for WiLDCOAST, a coastal conservation organization based in Imperial Beach. She misses LA often but suspects San Diego may be stuck with her.

Scott Barbour is a member and volunteer for San Diego Writers, Ink. He is co-facilitator of Room to Write, a drop-in writing group at the Ink Spot.

Judith (Judy) Barkley taught English at Grossmont College for too many years to disclose! Immediately upon retirement, she began taking classes in poetry writing from some of San Diego's finest poets: Ruth Anderson, Steve Kowit, Ryan Griffith, Sydney Brown, and Karen Kenyon. She thanks them for their instruction and encouragement.

Shannon Bates is a San Diego writer and musician with a love for all things green. When she is not writing fiction or playing her saxophone with local bands, she is editing for a music publisher, playing soccer three times a week, or making jewelry and gifts from repurposed materials.

Anthony Bonds hails from Texas, but has enjoyed a five-year (and counting) vacation in San Diego where he works as an editor and is learning to play the banjo. His first book, *The Moonflower King*, was published by Calypso Editions in early 2012.

Jim Brega, a native of San Diego, earned a BA degree from SDSU and an MFA from the University of Illinois. After a twenty-five year exile on the east coast, he returned to San Diego in 2008 and has recently finished writing and editing the catalog for a large local corporate art collection.

William Cass has had over thirty short stories accepted for publication in mostly smaller literary journals and anthologies, including *A Year in Ink, Vol. III*. He lives and works as an elementary school principal in Coronado, CA.

Janice Coy is a native Southern Californian who was raised in Oakland. She is a SCUBA diver, but prefers the warmer waters of the Southern Hemisphere. Jade Cove is her first published short story. More about her writing career as a journalist and author can be found at www.janicecoy.com

Jackson Crow-Mickle is a recent graduate of Bucknell University, where he majored in Creative Writing and European History.

Originally from the Chicago area, **Megan Elliott** now lives and writes in San Diego.

Richard Farrell is the Non-Fiction Editor at *upstreet* and a Contributing Editor at *Numéro Cinq*. He is a graduate of the U.S. Naval Academy and Vermont College of Fine Arts. His work, including memoir, craft essays, and book reviews, has been published at *Hunger Mountain* and *Numéro Cinq*.

Corinne Goria is Assistant Editor of Underground America, and Editor of a forthcoming book on human rights in the global economy from McSweeney's Voice of Witness. Her multimedia work, FromThenOnFire, was recently exhibited in the 2011 & Now Festival, and she is currently at work on the novel, *October Sun*.

Debbie Hall is a writer whose poetry has appeared in *City Works 2009 Literary Journal*, and whose essays have appeared on NPR (*This I Believe* series), in *USD Magazine* and the *San Diego Union Tribune*. She works as a pediatric psychologist at the Naval Medical Center, San Diego, California.

Judith Hansen began her working life as an actress and has performed onstage in New York and Los Angeles. One year after meeting an Irish rugby player named Phillip in lower Manhattan, she moved to New Zealand to marry him. Judith currently works in a more stable profession as a paralegal, to better support their two dogs, McManus and Sweetwater.

Linda Hutchison is a freelance writer living in La Jolla. She is the author of two books, *Lebanon* and *Finland*, for high school students. Her poems have appeared in *A Year in Ink, Vol I, The San Diego Poetry Annual, Urban Spaghetti, California Quarterly*, and *Magee Park Poets Anthology*.

Una Nichols Hynum was most recently published in *A Year in Ink, Magee Park Anthology, Oasis Journal, San Diego Poetry Annual, Spillway*, a finalist for James Hearst Poetry Prize, *The Writer's Digest* and *Margie*.

A former journalist and college instructor, an author of two prize-winning chapbooks and a widely published poet, **Oriana Ivy** was born in Poland and came to the United States when she was 17. She has been published in *Poetry, Ploughshares, Best American Poetry 1992, Nimrod, New Letters, American Poetry Review*, and more.

Marianne S. Johnson is married with two children, and a practicing attorney in San Diego who loves the desert. Her poetry is published in *Calyx, Sport Literate*, and in the anthologies *Lavanderia*, and *Mamas and Papas*, as well as *A Year in Ink, Vol. III* with San Diego Writers, Ink.

Brian Peyton Joyner pulled up his South Carolina roots twenty years ago, but his fiction remains firmly planted in the red clay soil of his birthplace. Brian lives in San Diego with his supportive husband and two perfect dogs. He is grateful to the writers of the Get It Published Writing Group.

Martha Kinkade is dedicated to promoting a peaceful and harmonious way of living. In her first book of poems, *Winter's Light*, she writes about her experiences growing up in Wyoming. Her poetry has appeared in Psychic Meatloaf. She lives with her daughter and teaches at San Diego State University.

Denise Kinsley received her BA in Arts and Letters and is an MFA candidate at Naropa University's Jack Kerouac School of Disembodied Poetics. She is currently working on a collection of short stories. Denise lives near the beach in north county San Diego.

Nancy Klann has had several short stories published, and also received numerous awards for writing. At past San Diego Book Awards, she won two prizes in the unpublished short story competition and first place for Best Unpublished Novel. She holds Excellence in Writing awards from the Santa Barbara Writing Conference.

Eber Lambert has written flash fiction, poetry and humor for 30 years for creative diversion and attempted sanity. He hosts New Poetic Brew open mic in South Park and has helped produce DimeStories in San Diego for over six years. His unfinished novel continues to haunt him from the attic.

John Farrell MacDonald is a chip engineer by day and a writer and editor by night. A member of San Diego Writers, Ink, since 2006, his works are in *A Year in Ink, Volume 2*, and in *Los Bilingual Writers Anthology, Book IV*. He is the editor of the blog at www.chip101.com.

Seretta Martin, a featured poet in the 2011 Border Voices Poetry Anthology and ITV show, is on the editorial staff of Poetry International and San Diego Poetry Annual; and hosts poetry at Upstart Crow Bookstore. A poetry teacher, she authored *Foreign Dust Familiar Rain*. Her writing appears in *Web del Sol*, *Margie* and other anthologies.

Chau Matser is a writer and artist who works in ink, watercolors and pen. She began writing stories at age ten but then broke up with it to see other people. She reunited with writing as an adult, and they are now happily married with two children. www.chaumatser. com.

Carrie Moniz is a poet and artist from the San Francisco Bay Area. Her work has appeared or is forthcoming in *Ploughshares*, *Third Wednesday*, and *Yellow Medicine Review*, among many others. She works as a senior editor for *The California Journal of Poetics* from her current home in San Diego.

Regina Morin is a long-time resident of Ocean Beach. An original member of the Border Voices Poetry Project, her poems have appeared in *Visions Magazine, America, No-Street Poet's Voice, San Diego City College Anthology, the San Diego Writer's Monthly, McGee Park Poets Anthology, A Year in Ink, San Diego Poetry Annual* and *The Reader*.

Susan Norton's poems have been published in over 80 literary journals, magazines, anthologies, newspapers, greeting cards, two art exhibits, a cruise brochure, tear off calendar, even in fortune cookies and read on NPR radio. She has received 10 writing awards, and with partner, Susan Dawson, has published seven childrens books.

Douglas Payne is a twenty two year old writer from Lemon Grove, CA. His work has appeared previously in *Breadcrumb Scabs* and *Mastodon Dentist*.

Judy Reeves has published four books on the craft including *A Writer's Book of Days*, the Revised Edition of which was named Best General Nonfiction in the 2011 San Diego Book Awards. She is grateful for the Brown Bag group and Thursday Writers where many flash fictions get ignited.

Nancy Sandweiss

Jennifer Simpson currently lives in Albuquerque, New Mexico where she is finishing her memoir *Reconstructing My Mother*, the last step towards her MFA. She also hosts the Albuquerque chapter of DimeStories. Her work has been published in literary journals, trade journals and community papers. This is her first poetry publication.

Karen Stromberg favors the short poem, flash fiction and the ten-minute play. Samples of her work can be found on-line at *qarrtsiluni, Pedestal Magazine, Red River Review* and elsewhere. She has been nominated twice for the Pushcart Prize.

Elizabeth Trude is a housewife and homeschooler. In addition to being all writerly and such, she is the crafty type and so is usually found tucked away in her "studio" drinking beer while covered in inks, glues, paints, threads...

Susan Union's feature articles have appeared in numerous newspapers and magazines. Susan has recently completed her first novel, *Moonblind*, and is at work on her second. She lives in Encinitas where she writes and teaches guitar. Find out more about Susan at www.susanunion.com.

Nicole Vollrath earned her MFA at Emerson College in Boston. Her recent short fiction can be found in *A Year in Ink, Vol. IV, San Diego City Beat* and *The Frozen Moment* forthcoming from Publication Studio. She teaches Creative Writing at UCSD Extension and cohosts "Room To Write" at San Diego Writers, Ink. www.sandiegowriters.org is her favorite website.

Editors

Brandon Cesmat is a practicing professional of the spoken and written word. He performs around San Diego as a member of the arts ensemble Drought Buoy and his books include *When Pigs*  *Fall in Love, Light in All Directions* and *Driven into the Shade*. He has won several San Diego Book Awards, San Diego Press Club Awards and been nominated for the Pushcart Prize. He recently served as artist-in-residence for the San Diego Art Institute's Page-to-Canvas-to-Stage program. He edited Classrooms of Poets, an anthology on teaching poem writing for K-12. He also teaches literature and writing at CSU San Marcos. His song "Between Blues" (adapted from Light in All Directions) has qualified him for the 2011 San Diego Songwriting Finals. He is published or anthologized in *ONTHEBUS*, *The San Diego Reader*, *Phantom Seed*, *Weber: The Contemporary West*, *Yosemite Poets*, *Don't Blame the Ugly Mu*g and the *Mamas & Papas*. He performs regularly at The Wine Pub in Pt. Loma and at Heaven Sent Desserts in North Park.

T. Greenwood is the author of six novels. She has received grants from the Sherwood Anderson Foundation, the Christopher  Isherwood Foundation, the National Endowment for the Arts, and, most recently, the Maryland State Arts Council. *Two Rivers* was named Best General Fiction Book at the San Diego Book Awards last year. Four of her novels have been BookSense76/IndieBound picks; *This Glittering World* is a January 2011 selection.

She teaches creative writing at both UCSD's Extension Program and at The Ink Spot. She and her husband, Patrick, live in San Diego, CA with their two daughters. She is also an aspiring photographer.

More information on T. Greenwood can be found at her website: http://www.tgreenwood.com and her blog: http://www.mermama.blogspot.com.

*S*an Diego Writers, Ink is a nonprofit literary organization that nurtures writers and those wishing to explore the craft of writing, fosters a literary community, promotes literature and celebrates artistic diversity.

The Ink Spot, located in the Art Center Lofts in San Diego's East Village, is our gathering place where we offer classes, groups, workshops, readings, and other literary events. The Ink Spot is also home to the Ink Spot Gallery, which features the work of local artists.

SDWI collaborates with other artistic, cultural, and community organizations throughout the city and county to promote literature and to inspire the community of writers.

We are grateful to The Merci Fund at the San Diego Foundation for its generous support and to T. Greenwood for her artwork.

San Diego Writers, Ink
P.O. Box 34374
San Diego, CA 92163

The Ink Spot
710 13th St., Studio 210
San Diego, CA 92101

www.sandiegowriters.org

Order additional copies of *A Year in Ink, Volume 1* (2008), edited by Thomas Larson; *Volume 2* (2009), edited by Sandra Alcosser and Arthur Salm; *Volume 3* (2010), edited by Roger Aplon and Jennifer Silva Redmond; *Volume 4* (2011), edited by Jericho Brown and Laurel Corona; and *Volume 5* (2012), edited by Brandon Cesmat and T. Greenwood at our website.

www.ingramcontent.com/pod-product-compliance
Lightning Source LLC
Chambersburg PA
CBHW060125260626
47160CB00005B/2024